Killing at the Kite Fair

Copyright © 2024 by London Lovett

All rights reserved.

No part of this book may be reproduced in any form or by any electronic or mechanical means, including information storage and retrieval systems, without written permission from the author, except for the use of brief quotations in a book review.

ISBN: 9798332591877

Imprint: Independently published

KILLING AT THE KITE FAIR

FROSTFALL ISLAND
COZY MYSTERY SERIES

LONDON LOVETT

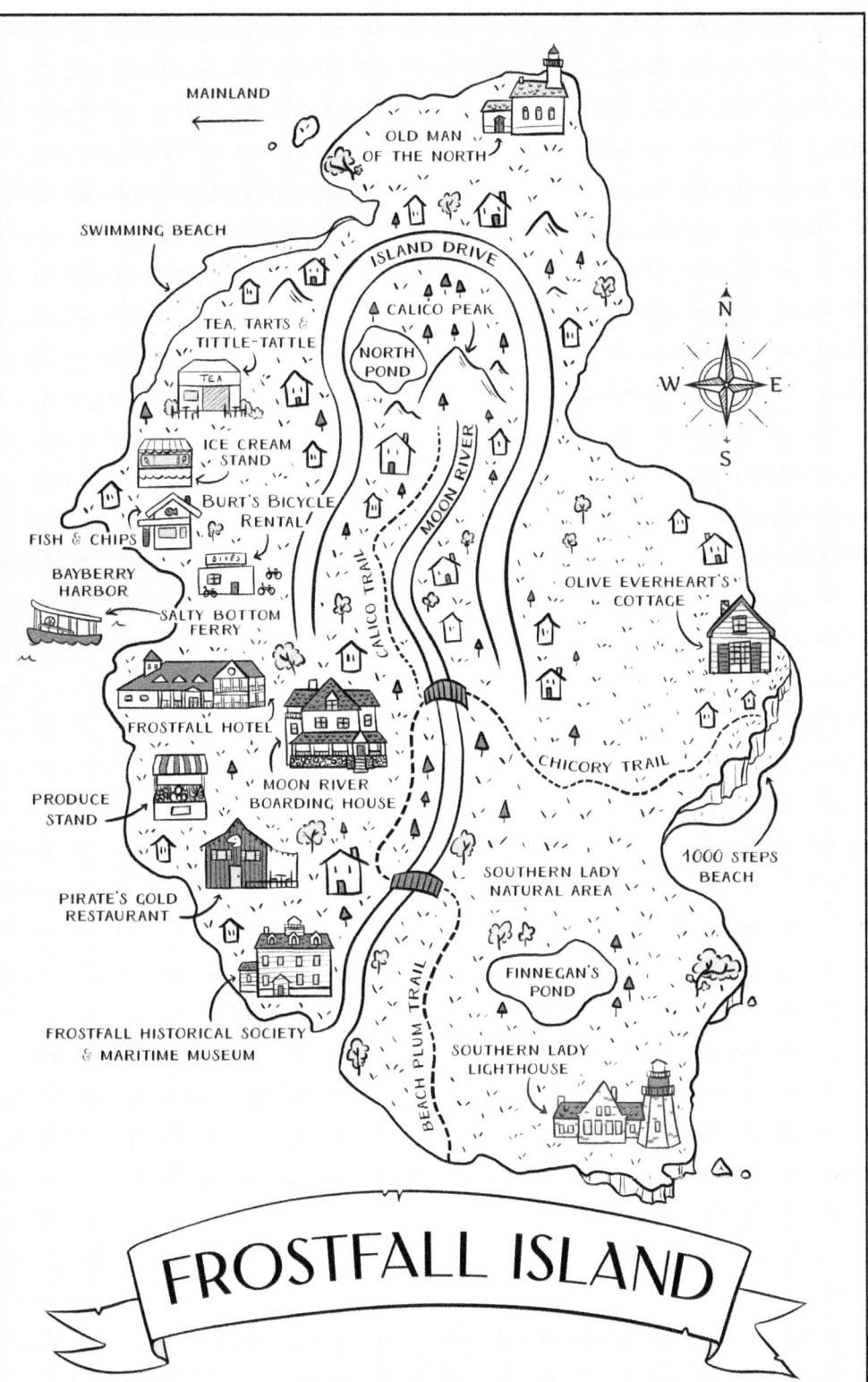

one

IT STARTED as a ripple of air, a blip in the space continuum, a disturbance so small it could easily have been missed. But I hadn't missed it. I'd felt it crawl right up my spine, but when I looked around—there was nothing. No one was there. It was just me, my dog, Huck, and the beautiful stalk of golden toadflax I'd been painting since the first flickers of dawn. In summer I had to get up extra early to catch that special moment when that great star we call the sun winked off the horizon before showering its glow and heat over Frostfall Island. I preferred the inconsistent shadows of dawn for my artwork. Watching nature wake up to a new day helped bring the plants to life in my paintings.

   I squinted out toward the vast ocean. It was smooth this morning, like deep emerald glass. The air was still, too… other than the mysterious ripple. The inexplicable disturbance happened more often than I liked, that feeling that someone was watching me from somewhere in the lush landscape. It was easy enough to explain away as a gray catbird staring across the trail at me from his shrubby hiding place, or a merlin perched high in a spruce while waiting for the pesky human to leave his hunting grounds, but I'd been on the island for nearly nine years, and I knew when an animal was lurking nearby. This ripple had been something more than that.

   Huck came bounding across the trail, having sufficiently dislodged a flock of robins from their roost in a nearby bayberry bush. He barked once to remind me it was time for breakfast. This morning, we'd decided to hike along the Beach Plum Trail. The bundle of toadflax I was painting bloomed right near the edge of the cliffs. I'd sandwiched myself between the Southern Lady Lighthouse, one of two island lighthouses, and the mouth of the Moon River, giving me an unobstructed view of the mighty Atlantic Ocean. I'd first come to the island as a brimming-with-joy newlywed and unabashed city slicker. But I gave up my apartment (where neighbors were so close you could hear them sneeze through the walls), my job in the business world (where every day brought a new headache and layer of stress) and the convenience of driving to the corner to buy anything I needed, from cough syrup to a new telephone charger, for the man I considered my soulmate and for a new life on an island off the eastern seaboard. Back then, I was the wife of a fisherman, learning how to adjust to a drastic change of lifestyle. As I grew to love life on the island, my marriage seemed to be going in the opposite direction. At least, I could see that now. There were subtle hints that Michael was unhappy, not as devoted, more distracted, but I'd refused to see it. I was sure I could make him happy, and we'd be together forever on our lovely island. Then one day he vanished from his fishing boat, never to be seen again. But lately, things had happened that knocked me off balance. I was starting to worry that there had been far more to Michael's disappearance than an unfortunate accident on a fishing boat.

Huck raced ahead, assuring me my time to dawdle was over and he needed his breakfast. My boarding house family would need theirs as well. I'd made a savory bread pudding for breakfast. It had soaked all night in eggy goodness and was ready to be baked to perfection. The Moon River Boarding House, a Victorian beauty with strong roof lines, a massive front porch and character-filled wrinkles, loomed over the landscape as Huck and I reached the bridge. A heavy snowpack sent the river rushing fast and furiously between its banks, and I could feel a cold spray of water on my bare legs as I crossed the bridge.

Tobias, a beloved member of my quirky boarding house family, was coming from the opposite direction. He had a towel over his shoulder and a floppy white hat pulled low over his head. Tobias took a long swim at the beach every morning, come rain or shine or even snow. It kept him fit and trim.

"Anna, how was the morning art session?" he asked.

I lifted my pad of paper. "Met a very cooperative stalk of toadflax. It turned out nicely."

We both reached the back door at the same time. "You should pull your paints out for this weekend's kite fair. I saw a few of the participants getting off the ferry with their kites. It should be quite the colorful display."

"That sounds like a good idea, although it's much easier to paint things that stand still." I opened the door, and Huck shot in ahead of us. We both laughed at his eagerness. "I suppose the island is going to be at full capacity this weekend."

Tobias took the towel from his shoulders and hung it on the step railings. "They were already setting up down at the swim beach."

The National Kite Club had chosen Frostfall Island for their annual summer fair. It was going to bring a nice surge of tourists and business to the island. My close friend Sera Butterpond had been baking tarts for days to serve in her tea shop, Tea, Tarts and Tittle-tattle—or the 3Ts, as we locals affectionately called it. I was particularly enamored with her vanilla cream and apricot tarts, a new creation that really showcased her talent as a pastry chef.

Cora, my sister and the most expensively dressed tenant in the boarding house, was wearing a pink silky number, a sleeveless dress that shimmered with every movement and showed off her tanned shoulders as she sipped her coffee at the table. The dress and the bright pink pumps on her feet were her attempt at casual summer wear. She came to the island with trunks full of designer duds and not much else. The expensive clothes were the only souvenirs left from being married twice to aging billionaires. Prenuptial agreements and very astute, greedy relatives of each dead husband made sure that was all she got. She did, however, have two incredibly lavish weddings, which, knowing my older sister as I did, made the whole thing worth it.

She sighed mournfully into her cup. "Why are there so many events on this island? I think we'd have more peace and quiet if this house sat in the middle of New York City. And kite people," she scoffed. "Something tells me grownups obsessed with flying paper dragons and butterflies on strings are not going to be big tippers." Cora had finally landed her first job...ever. She served tea and tarts at Sera's shop.

I pushed the savory bread pudding into the hot oven and poured myself a cup of coffee. "Breakfast in thirty," I called toward the stairs. Opal, a tenant who I also considered a best friend, came out of her room. A bold-print house dress fluttered around her legs as she plodded down the stairs in fluffy slippers. Cora was entirely overdressed for life on the island, and Opal was at the other end of that spectrum. She'd retired from teaching years earlier and had decided to take the word *retirement* to a whole new level. She spent most of her time watching black-and-white vintage classic movies. She was sure she'd been Rudolph Valentino in a past life, and who were we to argue?

Another door upstairs opened and shut, and heavy footsteps sounded on the stairs. These footsteps made my heart flutter, and, no matter how hard I tried, I couldn't keep the blush from my cheeks. Nathaniel Maddon was my newest tenant, and after a rough start and a few weeks where I considered telling Nate to pack his bags, I'd grown more than a little fond of the man. The feeling was mutual. Nate had left his job as a homicide detective on the mainland to find some happiness and solitude. Since his arrival on Frostfall, he'd worked on the construction crew in charge of restoring both of the island's lighthouses. Those projects were now finished, and he had some much-needed time off. Nate hoped to continue with the construction crew, only that would mean working on the mainland and that worried me plenty. He could travel back and forth on the ferry, but that could get old, fast. I hoped our relationship was enough to keep him ferrying back on that boat to come home to me.

Nate stepped into the kitchen and winked at me from the sideboard as he poured himself coffee. I'd cut up some melons as a cool, fresh starter for breakfast. I placed plates of honeydew, cantaloupe and crenshaw on the table.

"Hmm, that fruit smells delicious," Opal said as she picked up some cantaloupe. "Has anyone heard from Winston?"

Winston had boarded with me for over two years, but he'd recently eloped with his fiancée Alyssa. The young couple ran the local wildlife rescue. They'd considered having a wedding and then decided to save money and time by eloping.

"I think they're back this weekend," I said as I sat for some of the melon.

"I guess we're going to have a new boarder soon," Cora said with a little twinkle in her eye.

Opal laughed. "Yes, it'll probably be a tall, handsome billionaire who is looking for a new wife because that kind of person is always looking for a spare room."

"Hey," Nate said, pretending to be offended.

Opal laughed. "Well, I guess tall and handsome is a possibility, but I'm pretty sure the billionaire part is out."

"Are you packed and ready for your weekend?" I asked Nate. He was heading to the mainland for some mountain biking. I was glad he had time off to have fun on his bike, and at the same time, I would have loved to have him all to myself for a few days. I tried not to take it personally.

"I still have to do a little maintenance on my bike." He smiled at me over his cup of coffee. "Sure I can't interest you in coming? We could rent you a bike, and you could avoid the kite crowd."

"When I ride a bike, I like smooth, solid ground beneath my tires, not rocks and slippery mountainsides. Besides, I'm looking forward to the kites."

Cora groaned into her cup of coffee. "Kite people," she muttered.

Everyone laughed.

"I think I'll make some lemon bars," I said. "That sounds like a good dessert to go with kites." I smiled teasingly at Nate. "I might save you a few."

two

AS EXPECTED, Sera's tea shop was packed with customers, mostly unfamiliar faces. Her tables out front were filled as well, and my sister was hurrying around refilling tea cups and doling out tarts. She'd barely given me a glance as I walked through the table area.

"You're lucky you know the owner," Sera quipped as she spotted me at the counter. "I saved you an apricot tart."

I'd eaten more than my share of the savory bread pudding, and bread pudding was never a light meal, but since Sera had gone through the trouble of setting an apricot gem aside, how could I turn it down?

"I'll get it for you in a second," Sera said and hurried away with a teapot. An attractive forty-something couple sat at the table closest to the door. He had wavy light brown hair held back by a pair of silver sunglasses propped on his head. He was wearing a bold print shirt and a smirk. His tea companion looked a bit younger with short blonde hair and bright pink lipstick. She didn't seem terribly happy with her tablemate. That only served to make his smirk more pronounced.

Sera's wonderful husband Samuel delivered the apricot tart while Sera took an order from a table in the back. "Did Nate leave for the bike ride?" he asked, rather glumly. Nate and Samuel had become good friends and, more importantly, mountain biking buddies. Unfortunately, the busy kite fair weekend made it impossible for Samuel to go with Nate this trip.

"I think he's working on his bike first." I glanced around at the busy dining room. "It's crazy in here, and the first kite hasn't even been flown."

"They're holding an exhibition on the beach this afternoon," Sera said as she walked up. She nodded toward the table with the couple. "That man in the blindingly bright shirt is Theo Martin, the president of the National Kite Club. He mentioned it to me when I poured his tea. As if Sam and I will be able to leave the shop today. Your sister is already grumpy about the crowd."

Right then, Cora stomped inside, took a wild swipe at the strand of hair that had come loose from her ponytail and marched past us. "More tarts. People want more tarts," she muttered as she swept past.

"That's good, because we happen to sell tarts," Sera called to her. She turned back to me with a questioning brow.

I lowered my voice so the customers couldn't hear. "Cora is convinced kite people will be poor tippers."

Samuel laughed. "Actually, she's probably right." He

tapped the counter. "If you see Nate, tell him I'm jealous, but I hope he has a blast."

"I will, Sam." He returned to the kitchen. Cora emerged seconds later with a tray of tarts. She was on her way out the door when the woman with Theo Martin stood up abruptly, nearly crashing right into Cora. We all held our breath for a few seconds as my sister swerved and twirled around to avoid a tart disaster. She'd managed to keep the tray upright and the tarts survived. Everyone in the vicinity, Sera and me included, gave her a round of applause. If there was one thing to snap my sister out of a sour mood, it was a round of applause. She held the tray, bowed gracefully and then flashed everyone in the shop her million-dollar, Grace Kelly smile. My sister knew how to light up a room without ever going near a light switch. Her frown was gone, and she happily pushed through the door to the patio tables.

I turned back to Sera. "There—problem solved."

Sera tapped her temple. "Already saving that trick for her next bad mood."

We'd been so caught up in the Cora show, we hadn't noticed that the kite president had followed the unhappy-looking woman out the door. They'd taken their little spat to the sidewalk in front of the shop. Some of the other customers paused their nibbles and sips to stretch up and gaze out the window. The couple had the attention of the folks at the outside tables, too. In fact, those customers had front row seats.

Sera and I remarked quietly on the tense body language. The woman waved her arm at the man and said some terse words before spinning sharply on her sandals and walking away. The man stood there for a second, watching her. His smirk had faded but not entirely. He shook his head as he combed his fingers through his thick hair. He ignored the people staring at him as he walked past the tables. This time it was Theo Martin who nearly ran into my sister. He took the time to apologize and give her an overlong grin before returning to the shop to pay his bill. He pulled out some cash, tossed it on the table, then walked out.

Cora entered the shop. She'd been out at the tables and most likely overheard the entire argument, so, naturally, Sera and I called her over. "Hey, what was the kite club president talking about with that woman?" Sera whispered.

Cora's day had now gotten even better. She leaned forward enthusiastically. "I was just asking that couple at the table closest to the sidewalk. They're with the kite club, and that was Theo Martin, the club president, and his longtime girlfriend, Lyla Rogers. Apparently, there's been some cheating happening on his side of the relationship. That's what I heard when they were out there exchanging words. She told him she could never trust him again and that she didn't want to waste another minute of her life on him. That's when she stormed off. I have to say, he didn't seem all that upset. He all but asked me for my phone number when he bumped into me out there. What a smarmy smile." Cora gave a little body shake to show us how much she disliked it.

"Now here's a smile that's anything but smarmy," Sera said as she looked past me.

I twisted around on the stool. Nate walked in with his

backpack hanging off one shoulder. His bike was leaning against a lamppost on the sidewalk.

Samuel came out from the kitchen. "Are you guys going to ride at Sunset Peak? I hear they made a new downhill track. Lucky you. Think of your ole pal in here rolling out pastry dough."

Sera lifted a brow at him. "I told you to go and that I'd manage. It'll be better than having to deal with a mopey pastry roller all weekend."

Samuel adored Sera, and he gave her a gracious smile. "No mountain bike trail is better than spending time with my honeybunch." It wasn't sarcastic. He meant it.

Sera walked over and kissed his cheek. "Thanks, honeybunch. Now don't forget to roll out that last batch of dough. I think we're going to run short on tarts if we don't bake another batch right away." Sera sighed. "At least they'll all be out at the exhibition this afternoon, so we'll get a break in foot traffic. Have fun, Nate." They walked away, leaving me and Nate alone.

Nate took hold of my hand. "I was hoping my honeybunch"—he shook his head—"nope, no matter how much I adore you, 'honeybunch' is not in my vocabulary. Anyhow, how about walking me to the ferry, so I can sneak in a proper goodbye kiss?"

"I never say no to a proper goodbye kiss—sweetums?" I tried.

He shook his head. "Don't think we're the 'sweetums' type either."

three

NATE WALKED HIS BIKE, but he still managed to hold my hand. He squeezed it tighter as we strolled together toward the marina and the ferry dock. My good friend, Frannie Bueller, and her husband Joe, a retired fisherman, ran the ferry service between the island and the mainland. To say they were crucial to the island's overall existence was an understatement. Unless you owned a boat or hired a private one, Frannie's quirky, lovable and mostly seaworthy SS *Salty Bottom* was your only way on and off the island. That wasn't to say there weren't plenty of other boats in the harbor, especially on a bright summer day like today, but for those of us with no ambition to be mariners, Fran's ferry was a lifeline.

The *Salty Bottom* waddled side to side in its slip as Frannie huddled nearby with some of the other boat owners. The conversation looked serious and tense. Nate noticed, too.

Nate leaned his head closer and lowered his voice. "If I

didn't know any better, I'd say the boat captains on this island were conspiring to raise prices together. After all, we'd be obliged to pay whatever price they asked considering it's a long, possibly shark-filled swim to shore."

I smiled over at him. "Have you been spending time on those silly conspiracy chatrooms again?"

"Nah, those got less entertaining and more worrisome over time." We reached Frannie just as the group broke up. "See," he whispered, "outsiders just ended the meeting."

I rolled my eyes at him. However, I was curious about the grim expression on Frannie's face.

"What's going on, Fran?" I asked.

Frannie's solemn expression disappeared, and she smiled. "Looks like someone is going mountain biking."

"Otherwise, I look awfully foolish pushing this bike around," Nate said.

I elbowed him. "You are full of spice this morning."

He laughed. "I guess I'm just excited about the trip."

I turned back to Fran. "Now, what's going on? You quickly changed the subject, so I assume that little captains' meeting was important."

"Well, it's nothing really." Her tone implied that it was *more* than nothing.

"Fran?" I prodded.

She huffed as if I'd begged her incessantly. "It's just there's a boat out on the harbor, and no one has ever seen it before."

I looked at Nate. He had the same reaction to the seemingly non-news as me.

"I don't understand," I said. "Why the serious meeting? It's probably one of the kite club members."

Fran forced a smile. "Yes, I'm sure that's it." Again, the tone didn't match the comment.

"Except you don't think that's the case," I added.

"It's just that usually when a new boat comes into the harbor, the captain checks in at the marina first, and there are usually introductions and small talk, you know, to make sure someone with nefarious motives hasn't pulled into the harbor. This boat is anchored offshore, and a few of the other boat owners said they saw a tall man with a black cap pulled low over his face and dark sunglasses. He didn't wave or introduce himself or bother to make any contact with the marina."

"That doesn't sound good," Nate said. "Maybe I shouldn't go to the mainland."

I scoffed. "Nonsense. We don't know anything about that boat out there. He might just have stopped on his way to the mainland, and he didn't want to take the time to check in at the island's marina. And it's sunny, so a cap and sunglasses seem appropriate. I'm sure he'll be moving on soon."

Nate didn't look convinced. Neither, for that matter, did Frannie.

"Look, what's the worst that could happen on our lovely island?" I asked, and then knew I shouldn't have.

Frannie and Nate laughed. Frannie nodded that she'd take the helm on the response. "Let's see—what's the worst that can happen?" She buddied up with Nate as she spoke. "Nate, what happened this winter during the storm of the century when we were all without power and knee-deep in snow and ice?"

Nate made a big show of tapping his chin as if he had to give it some thought. "Oh, that's right. There were two brutal murders, and the duo of killers nearly sent Anna off the island cliffs to certain death."

"And tell me, Nate, what happened when a new, talented baker came to the island with his delicious breads and brownies?" Fran asked.

"Did he end up dead?" Nate asked facetiously.

"All right," I said, "enough of the vaudeville act. And his brownies weren't all that delicious. So, we get the occasional murder on the island."

Another hearty laugh from both of them.

"Why do I feel like the odd man out here?" I asked with a pout.

Nate put his arm around my shoulder, pulled me closer and kissed the top of my head. "Sorry, *sweetums,* but you started it with your question."

Frannie raised a brow at me. "Sweetums?"

"We're just taking a few lovey-dovey nicknames for a test-drive," Nate explained.

"And I thought we already took that one off the list," I reminded him.

"I don't know. It could work in the right circumstances," Nate said.

"The right circumstances being an entirely different girl-friend." I was still not over the sting of their earlier chiding.

"Right, duly noted. 'Sweetums' is off the list."

"You'd be lucky to get 'sweetums,'" Fran said. "Joe calls me 'sugar buns.'"

I pointed at Nate. "Don't even think about it."

"Hey, Nate, why don't you put your bike on board? Passengers will be lining up soon, and we'll take off in about fifteen."

I walked Nate over to the ferry dock. He leaned his bike against a bench and pulled me into his arms. "And now, about that proper goodbye kiss."

It did not disappoint. I came out of it feeling slightly lightheaded. I straightened his collar even though it didn't need it. "Be careful and do not ride down that hill as if you are immortal with your hair on fire."

Nate's blue gaze always made my knees weak, especially when his arms were around me. "I'll go down at a granny's pace and get off and walk around each rock."

I tapped his chest. "You are ornery, so you better go and get all that energy out."

Nate looked out at the harbor. There were plenty of boats anchored offshore. I was sure Frannie and the others were just overreacting, but I sensed it was still worrying Nate. "Which boat are they talking about, I wonder?"

I looked over my shoulder. "You'd have to ask Fran." I swung back around. "But don't bother. I mean what are you going to do? Swim out there and ask him for some identification?"

"I wasn't going to swim, but I thought maybe Frannie could turn the ferry that direction—"

"Don't give it another thought. Go and have fun." I stopped any more of his worry with another kiss. We hugged goodbye, and I turned to leave.

Nate took my hand and pulled me in for one more hug. "Save me some lemon bars, *lovebug*."

I laughed. "Maybe we can just stick with 'Anna and Nate.'"

four

A HALF-DOZEN colorful kites danced in the breeze over the swim beach. As a kid I loved flying kites. My dad would take Cora and me to the toy store near his apartment, and we'd each pick out a kite. Cora always went for the frilly butterfly kites, but I liked the more menacing kind, like the Batman kite or the fiery red dragon. In the end, Cora's simple but frilly butterfly kites always worked best. Fortunately for me, she preferred to just watch the kites, so she always handed me her spool, and off I went with her kite while my scary dragon lay dead, crumpled and defeated in the dirt.

Kites had come a long way since then, and along with the traditional diamond-shaped kites on the beach there were some impressive geometric 3-dimensional designs. I had a few minutes, so I headed in the direction of the swim beach. The inconsistent rumble of the *Salty Bottom* was followed by one of its pungent diesel burps. I glanced back. It was leaving the dock and heading to the mainland. I missed Nate when he was away, but his homecoming always made up for it.

The sun looked a little jealous as it tried to compete with the kites for top billing in the blue sky. It had turned out to be the perfect weekend for a kite fair. Clear skies and just enough onshore breeze to keep the kites afloat without ripping them from people's hands.

The beach was dotted with a few tents where cold drinks and snacks were being served. Lyla, the president's girlfriend, sat at a table shaded by a giant yellow and green umbrella bearing the words "National Kite Club." She was checking in members and handing out kite-shaped nametags.

There were plenty of spectators, too. The kids stared up at the kites with awe, pointing out all the extra cool ones. I was especially drawn to a kite that was colored and shaped to resemble a scarlet macaw. I took a photo to show my friend, Olive Everhart. Olive lived in a quaint cottage on the other side of the island. She rarely left her cottage, so I visited her several times a week with leftover goodies from our boarding house meals. Olive owned Johnny, a scarlet Macaw who liked to squawk out the first lines of famous rock songs. He was a big hit online.

The man holding the macaw kite smiled when he saw me take a picture. He looked to be about my age, with dark hair and blue eyes. His sharp features and muscular build made him look less like a kite-flyer and more like an actor in an action movie. The woman standing next to him adjusted her shiny white sunglasses as she stared up at their kite. She looked a few years younger. Her curly hair bounced in the breeze. I walked over to introduce myself.

"Hope you don't mind that I took a picture," I said. "It reminds me of the scarlet macaw that lives on this island. I'm Anna, a Frostfall local."

The man used his free hand to point at his nametag. "Owen Perez and this is my fiancée, Sadie. Did you say there is a macaw on the island?" He glanced around as if he might catch a glimpse of the bird.

"Not flying free. He's a friend's pet. He's quite the sensation online because he knows a lot of rock and roll songs."

The couple both grew wide-eyed and laughed. "Johnny, the rock and roll macaw," they said in unison. "We love that bird," Sadie said.

"He lives here on the island? Wait, I remember reading that. I can't believe I didn't put those two things together." Owen moved closer to the water with the kite. The giant paper bird fluttered and dipped and soared gracefully over the shoreline.

"Do you think we could meet him?" Sadie asked.

I'd name-dropped myself right into a corner. Olive didn't mind the occasional visitor, but she enjoyed her reclusive lifestyle. Posting videos of Johnny online was one thing, but having his fans in her living room was another thing altogether. "His owner doesn't go out much. If I see her, I'll ask." It was the best I could do, and it was time to change the subject. "This must be a big deal for your club. I've never seen so many kites at the same time."

"We have this fair every summer," Owen said. "Some of us

were worried that there'd be too much wind on an island, but the weather seems to be cooperating."

"Oh look, babe," Sadie said with a wave of long fingernails. "Aaron Wright just showed up. Looks like he went with a dragon theme."

We all looked in the direction that her fingernails glided. A fifty-something man trudged with clumsy steps through the deep sand. He held tightly onto a shiny green dragon kite, complete with a long tail that ended with strips of shiny silver bows. The kite was impressive and immediately grabbed the attention of the spectators on the beach.

"Now if he can get the thing in the air," Owen quipped.

The extravagant kite reminded me of some of the fancy kites I tried to fly as a kid. The more complicated ones looked cool, but they weren't easy to get airborne. "It's a beautiful kite, but it does look elaborate for takeoff," I said.

There were so many kites up in the air now that the white-hot sand was bathed in cool, moving shadows. We watched as Aaron licked his finger and held it in the air to identify the wind direction. He had on a hat, but his fair skin already looked red with sunburn. He surveyed the area and chose just the right spot.

Sadie snickered. "You'd think he was launching a space shuttle."

We all had a chuckle over her remark. Aaron did seem to be taking this seriously, and the fact that he now had a huge audience might have been the cause. He slid a backpack off his shoulder, dropped it on the sand next to him and then held the dragon in front of him. When he launched the kite, its tail danced in the breeze, tracing loops with its shiny silver bows catching the light from all angles. There were a few harrowing moments when it seemed the dragon was going to go rogue and dash dangerously close to the heads of the spectators, but its large wings caught just the right draft, and it floated magically up to the sky. The spectators cheered and clapped.

"I guess Aaron is the hit of the fair," a voice said wryly behind us. We all turned. It was Theo Martin, club president. The title was embossed in gold under his name on the tag. "Looks like most everyone came out for this exhibition."

"Now that you're here," Owen said sharply. "I've got a few complaints."

"You usually do, Owen," Theo said. He favored Sadie with his smile. Cora was right. It was a smarmy one at that, but Sadie seemed to like it. I was sure I spotted a pink blush on her smooth cheeks.

"Well, I specifically asked for a room with a view of the harbor, but we ended up in a room with no view and no balcony," Owen began. "And what about these meal vouchers for one breakfast? I thought the club dues would cover at least a full dinner out with a cocktail or two."

Theo looked as if he regretted stopping to see Owen at all. "Owen, the hotel only has a finite number of rooms with views, and as I explained in the group email, it was first come, first serve. By the time you sent your RSVP, the view rooms were taken."

"I'll bet you have a room with a view." Owen gave his kite

a tug, and the parrot dipped for a bit, then caught a new rush of wind to go even higher.

"Naturally. I'm club president." Theo added in a chin lift as if his title was worthy of great respect. "And I was the one making the reservations. And as for the meal vouchers—as you might recall, the members voted for a 10 percent cut in dues last year. That left less money for the annual fair, and a free breakfast was all the club could afford. Now are there any more complaints, or can I walk around and greet others?"

Owen scowled at Theo's condescending tone, and I couldn't blame him. I did notice, however, that Sadie found Theo's curt reply amusing. She had to look away to hide that amusement. My own attention was suddenly drawn to something in the sky that was most decidedly not a kite. A green and black drone flew on the perimeter of the swim beach, keeping out of the way of the kites but also getting a nice aerial view of the exhibit.

I nodded politely and left behind the tense chat. The man with the drone remote was standing in the middle of some seaside golden rod. He was young, maybe thirty, with a loosely fitting button-down shirt and cargo shorts. He moved the remote back and forth as his thumbs thumped the control pad.

"I guess you'll have the best view of the whole spectacle," I said as I approached. "I'm Anna, Frostfall local."

He smiled. "Dirk Evans, official drone flyer at the kite fair. Not that they hired me to be here, but I live across the harbor, and I saw the flyer for the kite fair. Thought it'd be fun to capture it from the air. Then I can upload it to my blog. There are some nice ones, too. That dragon is my favorite."

"I think that one is the hit of the fair so far." I watched as his tiny robotic device buzzed back and forth in the sky. It was much less graceful than the kites but just as impressive.

"Watch this," Dirk said. The drone took off toward the ocean. It flew out over a group of seagulls that had landed for a float on the waves. The drone caught their attention enough for orange beaks to turn skyward. A few took off and landed farther away but most just figured it was an extension of the bizarre human activities on shore. The drone swept around the birds once, and then Dirk directed it back toward the beach. "It's called getting a bird's eye view of some birds." He laughed at his pun. "Hold on." He pulled out his phone, flicked his thumb around on the screen and then pulled up the footage of the seagulls. They were white dots undulating on blue water.

"I guess I've never seen them from this angle." I needed to stop by the produce stand to buy some lemons before Molly sold out. "Very cool. Well, enjoy your time on Frostfall. I'm sure your followers will love the kite footage."

five

I'D PROCRASTINATED ENOUGH with mysterious boat stories, kite soap opera episodes and learning about drones. I needed to get home and bake those lemon bars. I planned to take some to Olive. It had been a few days since I'd seen my friend, so a visit was overdue. The late morning sun assured us that it would be a hot day on the island. I needed to get my produce before Molly closed her stand for the day.

My phone beeped, and I pulled it out of my pocket. It was a text from Winston. "Alyssa and I are back on the island. We thought we'd stop by later for a visit. We've got some pictures."

"Yes, please, I can't wait to see you," I texted back. Suddenly lemon bars didn't seem like enough. I needed to make some cupcakes for their return. After all, it wasn't every day you got married.

I reached the produce stand. Molly Pickering had been running the Frostfall produce stand for twenty years. She started the business with her husband once they moved to the island. Bart died of cancer years ago, but Molly decided to keep the business going. Every morning, at the crack of dawn, with the local fishermen, she ventured out on her small boat, crossing the harbor to the mainland to the big produce market in town. She returned with all the choicest fruits and vegetables. I could smell the lemons and ripe melons long before I reached the stand.

Molly was standing under her umbrella finishing a text. She looked up as I reached her colorful, fragrant baskets. "I was wondering if I'd see you this morning. I spotted Nate on the ferry with his bicycle."

"He's going mountain biking with some friends this weekend. I need some lemons for lemon bars." I stood with hands on hips and perused the selection of fruit. "Winston and Alyssa are back on the island. I'm going to bake some cupcakes, but I want them to be fancier than the usual chocolate or strawberry."

Molly clapped once. "I have just the thing." She leaned down behind her stand and emerged with a bag of pistachios. "Just got these beauties this morning, and I haven't had a chance to put them on display."

"Pistachio cupcakes with vanilla cream cheese frosting," I said excitedly. "Perfect. I'll take two pounds of pistachios and six lemons." I busied myself picking out six lemons while Molly pulled out her scale and weighed the nuts.

Molly bagged the nuts as her phone beeped. She paused to look at the text and shook her head. "Boy, oh boy, it's quite the day out here on the harbor."

I was sure she meant the kites. "I guess you'll be able to see the kites from your stand. There are some really cool ones out there. These people take their kite flying quite seriously."

Molly nodded. "I've seen a lot of people walk by with their fancy kites. I know the whole event is centered down at the swim beach, so I should be able to see some of the high flyers. But I wasn't talking about that. Even though it's a big deal."

"What were you talking about then?" I asked.

She moved in closer even though we were quite alone. "It seems we have a mystery boat in the harbor, and the stories are making their rounds and getting more embellished with each pass." She laughed. "Sometimes I think we all spend too much time out here on the water. The salty air and sun are drying our brain cells. Still, it's always a concern when someone shows up and doesn't bother to check in at the marina."

"I heard all about the mystery boat this morning. Maybe a group should go out there and greet the boat owner. That would certainly help solve the mystery and hopefully put some of the angst to rest."

"I agree. I think that's being considered, but mostly people are hoping he'll leave quietly and then the whole drama will disappear. He's anchored pretty far out in the harbor and away from the other boats. Someone mentioned he had a small dinghy attached to his boat, so people are convinced the mystery captain will come ashore and cause problems. You know this island and its propensity to worry about trivial matters."

"Well, even Frannie was upset about it this morning, which makes it seem a little more than trivial. I think I'll walk along the marina and see if I can get a glimpse of the boat and its mysterious captain."

"Maybe it's the ghost of one of Frostfall's long-lost pirates coming back to find his treasure," Molly said with a laugh. It was true. Long ago, the inhabitants of Frostfall had concocted exciting tales of pirate invasions on our fair island. There was an entire floor in the Frostfall Historical Society and Maritime Museum dedicated to our history with notorious buccaneers. From what I'd read, most of it was overblown fiction, but it brought tourists to the island, so no one bothered to shut down the stories. Our mostly theatrical and enhanced history was one of the things I found endearing about the island.

I paid for my produce and took a quick detour to the marina. After all the excitement and frenzied talk about the mystery boat, I decided to see it for myself. In the distance, the kites were doing amazing acrobatics in the air. The wind speed was still working in their favor.

It was summer, so many of the boats that made their home in the marina were out on the water this morning. It was a perfect day for sailing or fishing or even a trip along the coast. About a dozen boats were anchored in the harbor. Many were clustered together so boat owners could chat and board each other's vessels for a cup of coffee or a glass of wine.

There were plenty of boats I'd never seen before, but that was always the case in summer. I wasn't sure why this particular boat had garnered so much concern. Then I saw it. No one had to point it out. Its hull was painted steel gray and the wheelhouse was black. It was plain, without some of the usual bells and whistles of the other pleasure boats. I couldn't see the back of the stern, so it was hard to know if the boat had a name. I could see why people were disturbed by its presence. It was anchored a good distance away from the rest of the harbor, and there didn't seem to be anyone on board. At least that was what I thought until I saw a flicker of movement inside the wheelhouse. It was too far away to see clearly through the glass windows, but it seemed a face was staring out…at me.

A shiver raced deep through my body. I had no idea why. I decided it was time to get home and bake cupcakes. I took off at a much greater speed than necessary, but I wanted off the dock fast. At least now some of the concern made sense. There was something not right, something unsettling, about that boat.

With any luck, it'd be gone by the end of the day.

six

TWO DOZEN PISTACHIO cupcakes sat on cooling racks as I made Opal a grilled cheese sandwich. "Those smell delicious," Opal said. She'd been working on a crossword puzzle while drinking a glass of lemonade.

"I figured we needed something special when the newlyweds dropped by. I'm going to fill them with pistachio cream and then top them with a vanilla cream cheese frosting."

"Can't wait to try one."

I placed the grilled cheese down in front of Opal. Sometimes I envied her easy, carefree life. She watched her movies, did her puzzles, occasionally checked in with friends, but for the most part, she just floated through each day in her comfy smocks and slippers, waiting for her next meal and the next bit of gossip to cross the table. I didn't bother filling her in on the mystery boat in the harbor because I was convinced it wasn't going to stay long.

"I suppose you'll need to advertise for a new tenant." Opal

brought up another topic I'd been avoiding. But she was right.

"I suppose so. I dread the tedious process of advertising and reading applications and checking out references."

Opal looked up from her plate. "The last advertisement brought you a bit of a surprise."

"It did indeed, but that surprise came with its own blast of stress. As I'm sure you remember, Nate's introduction into the house was not exactly peaches and cream."

"True, but it turned out wonderfully in the end. Did he get off all right?"

I sighed. I always felt it keenly when Nate was no longer on the island. "He's really excited about this trip." I went to the refrigerator and pulled out the pan of lemon bars. I gave the pan a quick jiggle to make sure they'd set firmly enough to cut into squares.

Opal lifted her face and wriggled her nose. "Lemon bars, too?"

"Yes, but these are for us. Would you like one with your lunch?"

Opal laughed. "Do you even have to ask?" She pushed her napkin to the middle of the table. "I don't even need a plate."

I sifted powdered sugar over the bars and cut a square for Opal. "I'm going to take some to Olive along with some of the lasagna I made last night." I picked up my basket. That alerted Huck that we'd be walking to Olive's house soon. He hopped up and headed to the door.

"Not yet, Huck. I've got to pack up the goodies first." I set the lemon bars in a container and cut a chunk of lasagna from the pan. I tucked in some homemade yeast rolls and a few squares of this morning's savory bread pudding. Huck was more than eager by the time I reached the door. Opal had returned her focus to her crossword puzzle. "See you later," I said.

"Have a nice visit."

Huck raced ahead of me to the bridge. He stopped in the middle of the bridge to bark at a few ducks that were floating aimlessly down the river, then he trotted off toward Chicory Trail. Olive's cottage had a wonderful location at the eastern edge of the island. It gave her an unobstructed view of the Atlantic Ocean.

I reached the trail. All spring there had been muddy spots to avoid, but now it had hardened into the dry, dusty ground of a hot summer. Even though the trail was parched, the surrounding landscape was still lush from winter's snowpack, followed in quick succession by heavy spring rainstorms. Tall fronds of cinnamon ferns lined the trail. A smattering of white yarrow and blue chicory dotted the landscape beyond the ferns, and beyond the wildflowers, a small forest of scarlet oaks and white pines provided shade and a windbreak for the wild critters.

Up ahead, Huck had slowed his pace considerably. Then he stopped and turned toward the trees. I expected him to dash into the landscape to chase a squirrel. Instead, he stood as still as a statue. The hair stood up on his nape, and a low growl rolled out. I reached him and looked in the direction he was staring. That was when I saw it—a slight movement in the trees that wasn't from a breeze or bird. It was bigger. I was done jumping at shadows and having the hair on my neck stand up at every movement of air.

"Hello!" I called into the landscape. Huck barked sharply, startling me enough that I nearly dropped the basket of goodies. I set the basket down on a large rock and plowed past the ferns and toward the trees. "Hello? Who's there? Show yourself, please. Are you lost? I can help." I threw out everything I could think of, but there was no answer. I reached the trees, but no one was there. I glanced around the clearing. Whoever it was, they were gone. I'd walked bravely into the landscape, but I felt plenty shaken by the ordeal. I hurried back to the basket before squirrels or birds got a whiff of the goodies. Huck was still standing on the trail.

"Thanks for having my back, buddy," I told the dog with an eyeroll. His fur smoothed back down, and once again, he trotted energetically off toward Olive's house and her jar of dog treats. (She kept them on hand just for Huck.)

Most of the adrenaline had dissipated by the time I reached Olive's cottage, but she sensed something was up the second she opened the door. Huck raced inside, but Olive stood in the doorway with a concerned look. "What's wrong, Anna?" She glanced past me. "You look as if you've seen a ghost." She realized then that we were still standing in her doorway. "Come inside, quick. Tell me what's happened."

"It was nothing really. Just my vivid imagination running away with me. Huck, too, for that matter."

"Oh, Huck, forgot all about you," Olive chuckled. She carried the basket into her kitchen and returned with a dog treat.

Johnny, the parrot, came swooping down from the window ledge and landed on the back of the couch. "Awk!" he screeched. "Anna, baby!" It was my own custom greeting that I'd grown to love. I sat on the couch and rubbed the bird's soft, feathery chest.

Olive sat next to me. She reached into her pocket and pulled out a peanut. Johnny grabbed it in his massive, curved beak and jumped down to the ground to eat it. Olive still had a look of concern on her face. "Now tell me, what happened to shake you up like that?"

"I guess it's all a result of what's been happening down at the marina all morning," I started.

"The kites?" Olive asked, confused.

"No, not that. The kites are marvelous. Someone has anchored their boat in the harbor, and there's been a great mystery and a lot of rumors around it. Supposedly, the captain hasn't so much as waved at another boat owner. He never checked in at the marina, and people are concerned. Apparently, he wears a dark cap pulled low over his face and dark sunglasses, and he's been hiding in the shadows, so to speak." I was blathering away, and I hadn't noticed the change in Olive's countenance until I stopped to take a breath. I reached for her hand. "What's wrong? Have you had an encounter with the man?"

She nodded, but then just as quickly shook her head. "Not directly, no. But yesterday evening there was such a lovely sunset, I decided to step outside and admire it. It seemed every hue of pink and orange was painted along the horizon. Anyhow, I heard a noise behind me, so I turned around. A tall, dark silhouette of a man appeared farther down the trail, closer to the boarding house. He had on a dark cap but no sunglasses. His face was shaded by the hat, so I couldn't really see him, but he saw me." She lifted her arm. "I swear to you every hair on my forearm stood straight up. He stared at me, so I hurried back inside and locked the door." Olive pressed her hand against her chest. "My heart was racing fast. Poor Johnny must have sensed it. He wouldn't leave my side the rest of the night. I finally worked up the courage to glance outside. It was dark by then, and I didn't see him anywhere. I talked myself into believing it was one of the summer tourists hiking the trail. But he sure gave me a fright." Her face blanched. "Do you think it's the man from the strange boat? Is that what you saw, too, Anna?"

I thought about the last few moments. I really hadn't seen more than a movement in the landscape, and I certainly didn't want to alarm Olive. At the same time, she needed to be wary of her surroundings and be extra cautious. "It might just have been an animal. I think I overreacted because of all the hullabaloo down at the marina. But Olive, make sure you keep your door locked, and call me if you hear or see anything that doesn't seem right."

"I will, dear. I'm glad you have Nate living in the boarding house. He's so protective of you."

I was about to let her know he was on the mainland for a trip but decided it would only worry her. But her mention of Nate and the stranger on the trail did make me wonder if I should have told Nate to stay. I quickly shook the thought from my head. I knew how to take care of myself. Besides that, I lived with a houseful of people. It was time to change the subject.

"Did I tell you? Winston and Alyssa are back from their elopement. I've made them some delicious cupcakes. I'll bring you a few tomorrow. They're pistachio with cream cheese frosting."

"They sound delicious." She seemed to be scrutinizing my face. "You're sure it was nothing out there?"

"It was just a movement in the trees. It could have been anything, even a bird." Unfortunately, my intuition was telling me it was much more than that, but I would keep that thought to myself.

seven

THERE WERE NO MORE hair-raising incidents on the way home, but I was just as happy to arrive safely in my cozy kitchen. I had some pistachio cream and frosting to make. I made myself a cup of tea, tied on my apron and got to work pulling out the things I needed. Opal came downstairs and stood in the kitchen looking somewhat confused. She spotted Huck at his water bowl lapping up the fresh water.

Her forehead lines deepened. "Did you go somewhere?"

A jolt of worry hit me. Had Opal had a memory lapse? "I went to Olive's." I put down the bag of pistachios and turned to face her. "Are you all right?"

"Me? I'm fine. I know you went to Olive's, and I thought it was an awfully short visit."

I'd been at Olive's for at least an hour, my usual visit duration depending on how busy my day was. "I was there for the usual time, an hour, give or take a few minutes."

Opal looked exasperated. She rubbed her forehead.

"Do you have a headache? I have some aspirin," I said.

"No, I don't have a headache. So, you were at Olive's this whole time?"

Now I was getting more worried but for a different reason. "The whole time."

She waved it off and chuckled. "Then it must have been my imagination. I could have sworn I heard someone out on the front porch. It was creaking under heavy footsteps. I thought you'd gone out there to have a cup of tea. Never mind. My mistake."

I sensed it wasn't a mistake, and she knew it. She'd heard someone. That adrenaline surge returned. "Did they knock on the door?" I asked.

Opal walked over to the teakettle to pour herself a cup. "I'm sure I was just imagining it, Anna. I'd dozed off on the novel I was reading, and something woke me up. My window was open, and I heard those usual planks on the front porch creaking, but like I said, I'd been dozing, so maybe it was part of a dream. Don't worry about it."

I debated whether to tell Opal about my incident on the trail. I was always torn between alarming or worrying my friends or keeping them informed in case there really was a cause for concern. I decided to give a few details. Opal was the least dramatic of my friends.

"There's been a strange boat in the harbor, and Olive saw a stranger last night around dusk. I'm sure it's nothing to worry about. He's probably here for the kite festival, but I'll make sure to lock the doors, even during the day."

"Can't be too safe," Opal said. "Especially with what's

happened across the harbor." She carried her cup of tea to the table.

"What happened across the harbor?"

Opal looked up from her tea with a grimace. It was obvious she didn't want to be the one to share the news. "So, you haven't heard?"

My mind went straight to Nate. "Has there been some sort of accident?" My throat was dry as I asked it.

"An accident? No. There's been another murder."

My throat got even drier. "The Pillow Talk Killer?"

"Looks that way. It came on as breaking news as I watched a talk show."

The news had shaken me enough after my already nerve-racking day that I decided to sit down with my tea. The cupcakes could wait. The notorious Pillow Talk Killer was the elusive serial killer that drove Nate to leave the police force. He'd been chasing PTK for seven years without success. The monster was aggravatingly good at not leaving evidence at a crime scene. The killer left eerily sweet messages in lipstick on his victims' walls. He broke in or sometimes just walked into the houses and apartments of women who were alone and in bed, then stabbed them to death and covered their heads with a pillowcase. It was the work of a true psycho, but a cunning psycho at that. PTK didn't strike often, but lately the murders had been closer together. The last two had sent Nate into a dark mood. He felt he'd failed the victims, and he took the blame every time as if he'd committed the murder himself. This would surely ruin his weekend. My only hope was that he was too busy and too far out of phone range to hear the news.

"You're worried about Nate," Opal said.

I nodded. Nate and I had kept his past as a detective secret for a while, but now the whole house knew he'd been a homicide detective on the mainland and that he'd spent years on the force chasing down the infamous serial killer. They also knew never to ask him about it or his career. It wasn't a subject he liked to dwell on.

"He was so excited about this trip. I don't want it to put a damper on his fun. Did they give any details with the breaking news?"

"No, it was the usual breaking news. A big splashy headline—'Pillow Talk Killer Strikes Again.' Very few details offered." Opal picked up her cup and then set it back down. "You don't think—"

I waited for her to continue.

She shook her head. "That's just me letting my imagination run off."

"What? Please, tell me," I prodded.

"You don't think that mysterious boat in the harbor is—you know—PTK? Maybe he's here on the island." She sat up straighter, then slumped. "That's ridiculous. Forget I said it."

As badly as I wanted to forget what she'd said, it was glued to my thoughts. Opal seemed to realize it.

"Really, Anna, I'm sure if someone was on the porch, they were lost and looking for someone to help them get back to the harbor. And, of course, the PTK isn't here on Frostfall. It's too small a place. He'd be caught in no time, especially with our island investigator, Anna St. James, ready to bring down the bad guys." She sat back with satisfaction, certain she'd put some of my fears to rest. I, on the other hand, wasn't quite so sure. Everything felt off balance, and something told me this ship wouldn't right itself until the mysterious boat was gone and the latest serial killer news had faded and been buried by other big headlines.

My phone beeped with a text. Just seeing Winston's name on the screen helped pull my focus to more enjoyable things. "We'll be there around four. I hope that's not too late. Someone just dropped off an orphaned baby seal at the rescue, and we need to get him checked out and settled in."

"Four is fine. See you both then," I wrote back. "I better get to those cupcakes. Winston and Alyssa will be here around four."

"Oh, good. I've got my gift wrapped and ready to go." Opal yawned. "Well, I think I'll go up and finish that nap I started. Or do you need my help with the cupcakes and by help, I mean a frosting taster?"

"You can certainly stay to taste, but I don't want to keep you from that nap."

Opal must have sensed that I was still tense from our chat. She walked up behind me as I poured pistachios into the food processor. She squeezed my arm affectionately. "When stuff like this happens, it's nice to live in a house with a lot of good friends."

I reached back and patted her hand. "That's so true, Opal. Have a good nap."

Opal left the kitchen. I stared out the kitchen window as I

waited for the pistachios to pulverize into a paste. It was perfectly quiet and serene out the back window. A pair of ducks had waddled up from the river and were taking advantage of a Huck-free yard to preen their feathers. If there was someone out there waiting to cause trouble, then they had seriously underestimated Anna St. James.

eight

I SWIRLED the last bit of cream cheese frosting on top of the final cupcake, then allowed myself to lick the bowl. I'd earned it today. I was still on edge enough that Tobias knocking on the back door startled me. I'd decided to take my own advice and lock the doors, even while we were at home. It was odd because we rarely locked the back door, no matter who was around.

Tobias's cheeks were pink from the walk home in the hot sun. "Anna, I didn't expect the door to be locked."

"I know and it's probably silly, but there have been a few incidents, and, well—I don't want to rehash old news. How was your workday? I hope you don't have to work this weekend. It's such beautiful weather, and the kite fair is in full swing."

"Funny you should bring it up. I was going to change out of my work clothes and walk down to the beach to watch the kites. I was an avid kite flyer in my early teens. Would you like to walk with me?"

I glanced at the mess I still had to clean. After the long morning, dirty dishes could wait. "I'll join you, Toby." I untied my apron.

"Great. It'll just take me a second to change into shorts."

A few minutes later Tobias and I were on our way to the kite exhibit at the swim beach. I made sure to lock the back door, and that didn't slip by him.

"So, why are we locking the back door?" Tobias asked. "Not that I take any issue with erring on the side of caution. You can never be too careful." We reached the trail that would lead to the swim beach. Some of the bigger, higher kites were dancing above the treetops. "Wait, does this have something to do with the mysterious boat in the harbor?" Tobias asked.

I chuckled. "You've got to love how fast news travels on a small island. And to answer your question—yes, it does, sort of. I'm not sure if there's anything to these frenzied rumors about the stranger on the boat, but—" I paused. "Don't mention this to Cora. I don't want to frighten her. Olive saw a strange man out on Chicory Trail near her cottage last night. Nothing came of it, and eventually, the man disappeared, but it unsettled her plenty. I think we're all hoping that boat will be gone soon. Where did you hear about it?"

"Abner left his ticket-stamping post at the museum to come across and inform me of the—and I quote—'treacherous-looking boat sitting off the coast.' He sprinkled in a few details about the captain looking menacing and unsavory, but

I figured since Abner spends half his day in a museum filled with animatronic pirates, he was probably exaggerating."

We laughed. It was true that Abner Plunkett, curator of the Frostfall Historical Museum, took his pirate displays very seriously.

"It's certainly busy on the walking path," Tobias said. "I suppose it was to be expected with people travelling back and forth to the swim beach." A woman with three little boys passed us. Each child held a kite. One boy was crying because his kite had snapped in two.

"We'll get some ice creams," the mother suggested. That seemed to do the trick.

"I lost many kites to accidents," Tobias said. "I had one kite break off its string and drift out onto a busy road. Three cars ran it over before I could reach it. Needless to say, it was confetti by that time." Tobias pointed up ahead. "Look at that dragon. It's magnificent."

Aaron Wright's spectacular dragon was swooping in for a landing.

"I saw that kite earlier. It's certainly a showstopper." We reached the swim beach. Most of the spectators had found viewing spots either along the shore or along the upper part of the beach where the cement path meets the sand. The beach itself was covered with kite flyers.

Theo, the club president, had brought out his kite. It was shaped like a fighter jet. It was impressive, but Aaron's kite still garnered the most attention, even now as it rested limply in the sand near his feet. Some of the kids on the beach ran over to get a closer look at it.

"Most of these people are using dual strings," Tobias noted. It was true. These weren't your average "toss the thing in the air, run a little and watch nature take over from there." The kite flyers were using multiple strings to guide their kites through the air. They moved up and down, left to right and anywhere the person on the ground wanted them to go.

"My dad used to take Cora and I to the park near his apartment. He'd hold the kite up, and we'd take off running until it got airborne."

Tobias smiled. "I'm trying to picture your sister running with a kite."

"Mostly I ran and she watched."

Tobias nodded. "That seems more like it." We stood with the rest of the spectators and watched the rainbow-filled display. There were a lot of kites in the air, but these were experts. There were a few near collisions, but, for the most part, they managed to stay in control of their kites. Something about watching the kites flying overhead felt calming, serene. At least there was a big bright spot to a rather troubling weekend. I hadn't even looked in the direction of the marina when Tobias and I walked the beach path. The farther from my mind, the better.

"Oh, look, a parrot kite. Isn't that a scarlet macaw, like Johnny?" Tobias asked.

"Yes, I took a picture of it this morning and showed Olive. She loved it." Owen had apparently pushed aside some of his grumpy complaints of the morning to enjoy the day on the beach. His fiancée, Sadie, was not out on the sand with him. I couldn't blame her. The swim beach was in full sun for most of the day, and the sand got as hot as lava after a long morning. I was sure the kite enthusiasts would be calling it a day soon, too.

I looked across to Theo. His fighter jet seemed to be doing well, but Theo was jerking on the string, causing it to do a few nose dives. I wasn't sure if that was on purpose, for show or if his big kite had drifted into an unfriendly pocket of air. Theo glanced behind him before taking some large steps back to put more distance between him and the kite. He was backing up toward Aaron, but Aaron was busy in his backpack. As he pulled out a granola bar, Theo's shadow fell over him. He yelled Theo's name to let him know he was behind him, but that didn't stop Theo from taking another big, heavy step back. His foot landed directly on the dragon kite.

I could hear the snap all the way across the sand. The beautiful dragon kite flopped like a dying fish, its head moving in a different direction from its body. There was a collective gasp on the beach.

Aaron stood from his crouch. The granola bar slipped through his fingers, and he stared in shock down at his broken dragon kite. Theo didn't seem the least bit contrite about what he'd done. He even compounded the whole thing by lecturing Aaron. "You shouldn't leave a kite in the middle of the beach."

Aaron finally found his tongue. He looked straight at Theo. Theo's kite didn't seem to be having any aeronautics issues now. It was soaring above everyone's heads, but most people were too engrossed in the scene happening at ground level. The beautiful dragon kite had flown his last flight.

"You did that on purpose, Martin," Aaron accused Theo. "You've been jealous of my dragon since I carried him onto the beach. You saw your opportunity to destroy it, and you took it. It's always like that with you. If you're not the center of attention, then you manipulate things to make sure you are. You've got a terrible character. Always have."

The whole conversation was going in a much darker direction than I'd anticipated. It seemed this wasn't the first time Theo had done something like this.

"It did seem to be planned," Tobias muttered next to me.

I nodded. "I thought that at first, then I thought no, the president of the club wouldn't be that kind of a person. But now, it seems, I was wrong. He is that kind of a person."

"That man who stepped on the dragon kite is the club president?" Tobias asked.

"Yes, but something tells me he might not be after the next election. I already heard someone else complaining to him about accommodations and inadequate meal vouchers."

"Who knew there could be so much political discourse in a kite club?" Tobias said.

We both looked at each other and laughed.

"I suppose we should get back to the house. Winston and Alyssa are coming over with photos, and we'll have some cupcakes and give a toast to their future."

Tobias straightened his hat. "Then let's get back. I have a gift to wrap. Besides, I think I've had enough kite drama for one day."

nine

I FINISHED CLEANING up the kitchen mess and pulled out a three-tiered plate stand for the cupcakes. Unfortunately, I didn't have champagne on hand, but I made a big pitcher of lemonade. Cora walked in as I was setting out the wine glasses. I figured even lemonade would taste celebratory in stemware.

"Yum, what's the occasion?" Cora asked as she dipped a pinky into one of the cupcakes.

"Stop that. What are you, three? And I'm glad you're home. Winston and Alyssa will be here soon with wedding photos, and we're going to toast to their future."

Cora shot an amused grin at the pitcher of lemonade. "We're going to toast with lemonade?"

"Well, do you happen to have a bottle of champagne in your room?" I asked with irritation.

"If I did, I certainly wouldn't share it with all of you. And I stand by my earlier assessment that they rushed into this whole marriage thing."

A laugh spurted from my mouth. "This coming from a woman who leapt into not one but two marriage contracts before she'd even learned her groom's middle name. Winston and Alyssa have been working together at the rescue for nearly three years."

"Yes, but working together isn't being part of a relationship. They only started dating months ago. Anyway, I better go up and shower. What a day." She pushed a stray strand of hair off her face to give me a visual of just how busy the day had been. "Those kite people are an odd bunch, by the way. Lots of turmoil going on amongst them." She headed out of the kitchen. "And I was right—they're terrible tippers," she called from the stairs.

I knew Cora was mostly upset that she didn't get to help Alyssa and Winston plan a wedding. She had big plans for it. The moment she heard about the engagement, she started writing lists and gathering ideas from the internet. She was more than a little sour when she discovered that they'd decided to save money and time by eloping. There weren't enough reliable people to watch over the animals at the rescue, so Alyssa didn't want to be away for long. As it was, they only had time for a quick two-day honeymoon after the nuptials.

The treats were ready. It was late enough in the afternoon that I figured Nate had had his share of biking. I decided to check in and see how he was doing. I was hoping he hadn't heard the news about PTK yet, but with modern technology following us wherever we went, I doubted that was the case. The call went straight to voicemail. "Hey, Nate, just checking in. I hope you're having fun." I hung up, and my mind went directly to all the worrisome things that had happened. I wondered if the boat had left the harbor yet. I knew Frannie was extra busy today, so I'd text her later. She'd know whether the strange boat had left.

There was a knock on the back door. This time I managed not to startle. I hurried to open it. "Since when do we lock the back door?" Winston said with a chuckle. Winston's cocoa brown eyes sparkled with joy. His thick blonde hair was brushed back off his face and his skin glowed with a golden tan. Alyssa held tightly to his arm. The same look of joy sparkled in her eyes. Cora considered herself an expert on all things having to do with relationships and marriage, but she was entirely wrong on this one. The young couple looked gloriously happy.

"Come inside. I've made some pistachio cupcakes and lemonade."

"You shouldn't have gone through so much trouble," Alyssa said. She smiled at the cupcakes. "But I'm glad you did. Those look delicious."

The rest of the housemates trickled downstairs with their gifts, and we all sat down to eat cupcakes and toss out toast after toast with our lemonade-filled wine glasses. Photos were passed around. Alyssa had picked a beautiful, bohemian lacy dress with lacy sleeves and a matching lace veil. The couple got married on the side of a river, out in nature, their favorite place to be.

Alyssa was busy relaying details to Cora, who listened with keen interest. Winston and I had a chance to chat. We'd grown quite close in the past few years.

"You two look so happy, Winston, but we'll miss you around here."

"I plan to visit often." Winston picked up another cupcake. "Just text me whenever you're baking, and I'll be at the doorstep."

I laughed. "I see, so our friendship is based solely on my brownies and cupcakes."

Winston finished a bite of cupcake. "Your baked goods are the best. But seriously, Anna, thank you so much for making me feel so at home here at the boarding house. I'll miss living here."

"Well, visit anytime. And I'll make sure to shoot off a text when something particularly delicious is in the oven." A bout of laughter pulled our attention to the other side of the table.

Winston shook his head in dismay. "Alyssa is no doubt recounting the embarrassing moment when I couldn't find the darn ring. Looked in all my pockets and tore apart the hotel room. Alyssa told me to try my pockets once more and, sure enough, it was there."

Huck barked to go outside. "I'll let him out." Winston got up and went to the door. Huck wagged his tail excitedly and trotted out once the door opened. Winston stood in the doorway for a moment. "Go on. You asked to go out," he said.

Seconds later Huck came scurrying back inside with his tail between his legs. Winston shot me a confused look. I got up to check on the dog. My heart was racing for what seemed the millionth time today. Huck curled up on his pillow and tucked his nose under his tail.

"That was weird," Winston said. "He just stood on the top step, stared down toward the river and growled. I couldn't see anyone out there."

This wasn't the time to bring up the stranger or the mysterious boat. We were celebrating something wonderful. The others were busy listening to the elopement story, and I had no intention of ruining the mood with my worries.

"I'm sure he spotted a raccoon. He doesn't like them." I walked to the door, opened it and did a quick glance around the yard. I tried to make it look casual, as if I only expected to see a raccoon.

I closed the door and discreetly turned the lock. Winston was back at the table. I sat down next to him and forced a smile.

"It's pretty early for a raccoon to be out," Winston said. "It might be sick. Alyssa and I will look out for it on our way home."

It took me a good ten minutes to release the angst I'd been feeling about Huck's odd behavior. I knew my dog. He'd spotted something outside, and it wasn't a raccoon. We'd been having a great time, but I was somewhat relieved when Alyssa insisted they get back to the rescue. I packed them some cupcakes, and we hugged goodbye. On their way out, I pulled Winston aside for a second.

He expression turned to concern almost instantly. "Aha, I knew it. Something has you upset, Anna. What is it?"

"It's probably nothing, but Olive spotted a stranger

lurking around Chicory Trail yesterday, and there's a strange boat in the harbor. It has people a little worried. Just keep your eyes open on the walk back." His brow lines deepened. I hugged him. "Like I said, it's nothing, I'm sure. Just wanted you to be extra vigilant on your walk." I hated to end the fun celebration on such a dark note, but I wouldn't be able to live with myself if I hadn't warned him and something happened.

"That explains the locked back door. When is Nate back from his trip?"

"Sunday, I think." I hugged him again. "We're fine here. We're a big group, and we look after each other. And Winston—congratulations again. You deserve all the happiness in the world." We hugged again. His smile was a little less radiant as they walked out, but I was glad I'd told him. I might not have thought of it at all if it hadn't been for Huck. My dog was curled up on his pillow, his nose still tucked under his tail. Something had scared him.

ten

WE'D ALL FILLED our bellies with cupcakes and lemonade late in the afternoon, so no one seemed interested in dinner. Being set free from the dinner shift was just what I needed. I had a big mental sit-down with myself. It wasn't a bad thing to be cautious when something didn't seem right on the island, but it wasn't like me to cower inside either. I always felt better doing some exercise, so I pulled out my bicycle for a long ride. If a menacing stranger was lurking in the shadows, I wanted to know about it. If something happened, the locals would come to me for help, and I planned to be out ahead of the trouble. Nate hadn't called back, but I was sure I'd hear from him later.

The sun was low but still shining in the early evening. I could hear music, voices and laughter down at the harbor, mostly coming from visiting boats. Hearing all the revelry put me in a more positive mood. There were a lot of festivities and happy people on the island this weekend, so our mystery stranger was greatly outnumbered.

I drove along the path hoping to spot Frannie, but the sign on the ferry said closed. She was home for her dinner break. In the colder months with shorter days, that would be the end of the ferry rides on the harbor, but in summer, especially on a busy weekend, she and Joe kept the ferry running until dark. The wharf and marina were crowded. The kites had come down, and now the visitors were walking along the docks, looking at boats and enjoying the tasty treats on the wharf. There was no sign of the club president or Aaron, the man whose dragon kite was damaged.

I rode past the 3Ts, but they'd closed up for the night. I considered a short trip to Sera's and Samuel's place, but I was sure they were exhausted from the busy day. The last thing they needed was a visitor. I paused to look around at the landscape just in case someone was lurking behind the shrubs. The birds and squirrels were active because it was close to dusk, but no sign of a dark stranger hiding in the shadows.

Out of the corner of my eye I spotted Dirk's drone buzzing over the trail across from the swim beach. I hopped back on my bike and pedaled in that direction. Dirk was standing in a clearing near some yellow birch trees. It was hard to find the focal point for his drone mission. I didn't know anything about drones, but seeing Dirk's in the air had increased my interest in them. It was amazing to see how far technology had come, only I supposed a simple drone was already a relic of the past. Machines and artificial intelligence seemed to be moving at lightning speed. Much like Dirk's drone. It shot quickly sideways before lowering itself to the ground.

I parked my bike and walked into the clearing. "See anything interesting?" I asked.

Dirk jolted at the question. He spun around with a guilty look and a blush covered his face. "Uh, no, not really." He saw it was me and relaxed some. "Well, I mean, I'm not spying, if that's what you mean."

I shrugged. "Actually, no, that isn't what I meant, but I suppose when that drone is in the air, it can catch a lot of things, even things it shouldn't."

Another blush crossed his face. "Yeah, you'd be surprised at all the things that pop onto that feed. It's hard not to catch personal interactions when you're flying it in a public space." He looked at the surroundings. "And with all this thick landscape, there are plenty of secret spots for people to—" He shook his head. It was cute to see how deeply red he could blush.

"Well, that was a cliffhanger," I said with a laugh. "Nothing too wild, I hope. We try to keep our standards high here on Frostfall." I laughed again to assure him I was joking. Something told me his little airborne robot zeroed in on a tryst or a secret kiss somewhere on our fair island.

And that was when it hit me. Dirk and his drone had been recording the island and all its lush landscape. "Dirk, and let me preface this by saying I'm not trying to get you into any kind of trouble, but you've been recording a lot of areas on the island, right?"

"I've been all the way up to the peak. Got some really great footage up there. It's always fun to catch animals in their natural habitats when they don't know a human is watching. Of course, the drone sometimes scares them off, but most of the time, it works."

"This might sound strange—but did you happen to see any footage that—gosh—hmm—did you see anyone out here, in nature, hiking around, who looked like they didn't belong?"

Dirk's face lit up. "As a matter of fact, I did. It was yesterday in the late afternoon. He was on the east side of the island. I'd just come up from the beach. Boy, they named that beach right. It felt like a thousand steps. By the time I reached the top, I was breathing like I'd run a marathon."

"Yes, it's quite a climb." I was anxious to hear what he saw, but I didn't want to be rude. "Anyhow, you were mentioning you saw someone?"

"That's right. I reached the top of the steps and sent the drone off over the trees near the trail. Mostly, I was trying to get a shot of the island at dusk. It was working nicely, lots of shadows, and the animals were starting to take shelter for the night. Then, suddenly, there was a dark figure in the shot. He was wearing a cap on his head and sunglasses, even though the sun was already well past the sunglass stage. He seemed to be creeping around in the trees, all while keeping an eye on the trail. I think he heard the buzz of the drone overhead, and that sent him deeper into the canopy. I lost sight of him after that."

My muscles were tense with anticipation. "Did you by any chance save the footage?" I held my breath for his answer.

"Sure did. I keep most of my footage because sometimes I miss something important if I merely glance at it as it's coming in on my phone. I like to sit in my office at home, upload it to my desktop and really give it all a thorough look."

"I hate to be a bother, but I'd be very grateful if you could show me the footage with the man in the cap. My friend saw him earlier, and it worried her."

"I can't blame her." Dirk already had his phone out. His thumb was flicking over the screen. "Whatever he was doing, it didn't look good." He flicked his thumb a few more times. "Here it is. Let's move to the side. There's too much sun here to see the screen well, and like I said, he disappears pretty fast. I think he didn't want to be seen."

We found a shady spot, and Dirk started the video. "It takes a few seconds, but keep your eye on the right corner of the screen."

At first, the only movements were the tree branches and a few birds skittering through, then he stepped into view. The drone captured the top of his cap. It was black, and he was wearing a dark shirt and jeans. His shoulders were hunched, and he seemed to be looking through an opening in the trees. A few seconds later, he turned his face ever so slightly toward the noise above him. The glasses and hat bill hid his face well enough that it was impossible to see him. Just as Dirk said. Seconds later, he dashed out of view.

"Do you see what I mean? It looked like he was hiding

and trying to spy on someone or something," Dirk said. "Maybe he's a private eye."

"The island doesn't usually see too many of those, but you never know." I didn't want to let on that the short scene on his phone had left me shaken. There was something about the person, a man, I was certain, that made my legs wobbly.

"I'm sorry I didn't get a better shot of his face, but I have to say, I don't think he's from the kite club," Dirk said. "I spent the whole morning with them on the beach, and none of them were wearing dark clothes and a dark cap."

I nodded. The sun seemed to be setting faster than expected. It was time to get home. "Thanks so much for taking the time to show me that. Stay safe." I hurried back to my bike, climbed on and pedaled as fast as I could back home.

eleven

THE SUN SEEMED to be setting faster than my bike was traveling. It was almost dark when I reached the dirt path that led to the boarding house. A noise caught my attention, but it wasn't anyone lurking in the bushes. It was a flirty giggle. A low, deep voice followed. They were on the bridge that connected the Chicory and Calico Trails. Daylight had mostly evaporated, but I immediately recognized Theo Martin's bold-print shirt. His silver sunglasses were pushed up on his head, holding back his thick hair. The woman sandwiched between Theo and the bridge railing was not his girlfriend, Lyla.

The woman playfully pushed at his chest pretending she wasn't receptive to his advances. She giggled again, and as she did, her face turned up enough that I could see her. It was Owen's fiancée, Sadie. I moved on. It was obviously a private and secret moment. Was that what had Dirk blushing like a schoolboy? He'd started to tell me something about people in secret spots, but I didn't ask for more details. Now I'd seen the details firsthand. It seemed the club president had been seeing the fiancée of one of his club members. It brought back the scene this morning, outside the tea shop, where Theo's girlfriend, Lyla, had let Theo and everyone at the shop know she wasn't happy with him. Maybe Lyla already knew that Theo was cheating on her with Sadie. Did Owen know as well? Cora was right. There did seem to be a lot of turmoil for a kite flying club.

The stars were beginning to peek out of the freshly darkened sky as I reached home. I put away my bike and sent off a quick text to Fran as I walked to the house. "Is that strange boat still anchored in the marina?"

Her text came back quickly. "It was still there when I brought the ferry in for the night. Joe and I were just discussing whether to notify the Coast Guard. He thinks we should wait to see if it's still there in the morning."

I considered letting Frannie know about the stranger on shore, but Joe was right, the whole thing could wait until morning. Besides that, I had no idea if the man in the black cap had any connection to the boat. Maybe I was connecting dots that weren't really there. On the other hand, maybe those dots were there, and they were drawing a dangerous picture.

"I'm sure he'll be gone by then," I texted back. Of course, I wasn't the least bit certain. "Have a good night." I unlocked the back door and went inside. Huck was extra happy to see me. His tail circled like a propeller, and he even barked a few times. His exuberance was mostly due to his evening treat.

My sister, on the other hand, looked far less excited to see me. She was deep in thought as she stared into her cup of tea. A fashion magazine was splayed open on the table next to her cup of tea, but she wasn't looking at it.

I walked over to the treat jar and pulled one out for Huck. He carried his cookie to his pillow, so he could enjoy it in comfort.

"Why do you look so glum?" I asked. "Are you still upset about not getting to plan Winston's wedding?" The kettle was hot, so I poured myself a cup of tea.

"No, it's not that, although I still think I could have planned them a day they would never forget."

I sat down across from her. "Did you see how happy they are? They got married out in nature, and the photos were beautiful. I'm sure it was a day they'll never forget. Not every bride wants to arrive on a Cinderella-style carriage and have ice sculpted swans lining the reception area."

Cora lost that early pensive expression, and her eyes sparkled with an old memory. "That carriage was wonderful, wasn't it? And that dress—it was spectacular. I really did feel like Cinderella arriving at the ball."

"Except your Prince Charming was ninety years old, and his best man was an oxygen tank." My beautiful sister didn't need any help stealing the show. She could have arrived at the wedding in sweatpants on a scooter and still have made the same impact.

Cora huffed. "Why do you always ruin my good memories with—"

I laughed. "With reality?"

"Oh, shut up." She flipped through the magazine loudly and purposefully, even though she didn't seem to have any interest in the photos or articles.

"So, what's bothering you?" I asked as I sipped my tea. Since it was my sister and since I knew her so well, I expected her to complain about not being able to buy the latest high-dollar shoes or the newest five-hundred-dollars-a-bottle skin cream.

"It's nothing, really. I was just tired after the long day at work, so I'm sure I was imagining all of it."

I sat forward so fast the table wobbled, and my tea splashed over the rim of the cup. "What was it?" I asked brusquely.

She waved her hand. "Settle down. It was nothing."

"Tell me." I couldn't tamp down the aggravation, and it was mixed with plenty of angst.

"I shouldn't have said anything. Now you're in a big lather over something that was mostly just a weird feeling." She shivered once, which meant nothing because my sister was a pro at the fake shiver thing.

"Cora, I need to know," I said as calmly as possible.

Cora stared at me, assessing my reaction. Just as I knew her well, she knew me well, too. "Is this why we're keeping the back door locked all of a sudden?" Her eyes rounded. "Is that serial killer here on the island?" She pulled the edges of her cardigan close around her as if her cashmere sweater could keep her from harm.

"I don't think that's the case, but there have been some

sightings—" I started, then didn't know how to finish, but I had her full attention now.

"Sightings?" she asked and again fussed with her sweater.

"Olive saw a stranger on the trail near her cottage, and I saw some drone footage of a man who was lurking in the trees. I think it was the man Olive saw."

Cora relaxed some. "Then I'm not crazy. I was blaming it on the long day at work and then I worried that maybe living on this island was starting to—you know—make me nutty."

"You mean like those of us who've been here for years?" I asked wryly. "Sorry, but you came pre-nutty, my dear sister. What made you think you were crazy?"

"On my walk home, as I passed the bridge, I got this sudden creepy feeling that someone was watching me. Maybe we should ask Fran if the PTK came across on the ferry."

"How would Fran know it's the PTK?" I asked.

Cora shrugged and I knew I was going to get one of her ridiculous theories. "I'm sure a serial killer has to have a certain look about him, you know, shifty eyed with an evil grin. Fran sees everyone who comes to the island. Maybe there was someone suspicious-looking on the ferry."

"I'll text her to ask if she saw anyone with a shifty eye on her boat," I said facetiously.

"See, you're not even taking this seriously. I'm sorry I said anything." Cora picked up her tea and took a loud slurp.

"You're right. It's nothing to make fun of. And I'll walk you to work in the morning. Then you can text me when you're ready to walk home."

"I don't need a babysitter, and what about you being out there on your own?"

"I'll bring my bike along to ride when I'm alone."

Cora fidgeted with her sweater again. "Do you think there's someone dangerous out there in the woods?" She shivered again, but this one looked less forced. "Why don't you call Nate home?"

"Because he's having a good time, and I don't want to worry him. Besides, we can take care of ourselves."

Cora shifted her bottom on the chair. "Speak for yourself. If I had a hunky man like Nate in the sidelines, you'd better believe I'd be pulling out all the stops on my damsel-in-distress mode." Cora stood up and patted her hand over her mouth to cover a yawn. "I'm exhausted. It's straight to a bubble bath and bed for me. Don't forget to lock up," she said on her way out.

No way I'd forget that tonight. I checked my phone on the way to the front door. Still no message from Nate. I wasn't going to let that worry me—at least not yet.

twelve

I'D TOSSED and turned for a good portion of the night, and it was easy to talk myself out of the dawn art session. I would have skipped it anyway. It would be silly to make sure all the doors were locked, only to head out into a mostly dark landscape with just Huck by my side. And my dog had proved himself to be quite the coward when it came to strangers lurking about. Still, he was happy to venture out once the sun was up and solid in the sky. Whatever had frightened him on the back stoop yesterday, he'd forgotten all about it. I sometimes wished I could do the same thing. I hated being nervous while going about my daily routine. I didn't like feeling unsettled in a place where I'd always felt comfortable and at home.

A few clouds dotted the sky above, causing a slight drop in temperature. The breeze this morning was strong enough to make the trees ruffle. It would be another great day for the kites. The kites reminded me of the secretive tryst I spotted on the bridge. It seemed there was quite a soap opera happening behind the scenes of the kite fair.

Huck barked and I startled. "Ugh, Anna, stop being so silly," I muttered to myself. Still, I hurried down to the river to find out why my dog barked. A squirrel stood on his hind legs on the bank across the water. The river was zipping furiously along, so Huck knew not to cross it. The squirrel seemed to realize his nemesis was stuck on the opposite bank, so he waved his tail teasingly back and forth before running up a nearby tree.

I patted Huck's head and took a few steps backward. "Those clouds are nice," a deep voice said from behind. I didn't recognize it right away because the rushing river was making too much noise.

I gasped and spun around like a paranoid fool. Tobias frowned. "I'm sorry, Anna. I didn't mean to sneak up on you like that." Tobias adjusted the floppy hat on his head.

"No, I'm sorry for reacting that way. I guess I'm still a little jumpy." Understatement of the day. "How was your swim?" I wanted to add "Did you see any strangers hiding along the trail?" but I kept that to myself.

Tobias's brow turned serious. "It's not like you to let stuff like this get to you, Anna. Do you think we're in danger?" It was the first time someone asked me that directly and the first time I really thought about it. And the reaction that floated up from my intuition was not what I expected.

"You know, Toby, now that you ask it that way—I'm not

sure if it's danger I'm sensing. Let's just say *something* has me uneasy. I feel like something big is in the air, but I don't know what. My feelings are all over the place. It's as if there's something lurking nearby, something reminding me not to get too settled in my life." I shook my head. "Oh my gosh, don't listen to me. I didn't sleep well."

"I'm sure you'll feel more at ease once Nate is back." Tobias blushed under his already sunburned complexion. "I'm not big and tough like Nate, but I keep fit, and I won't let anything happen to you, Anna."

I touched his cheek. "I know you won't, Toby. Thanks. Let's head in. I made your favorite—hashbrowns and scrambled eggs."

"Wonderful. I worked up an appetite with that swim. The kites were starting to arrive as I left the beach."

I was relieved to be done with our earlier discussion. I'd been dwelling on it far too much, and I was starting to let the most ridiculous notions swim through my head. I needed to get on with my day and not think about it anymore.

We walked into the kitchen. Cora was dressed and ready for work, and Opal was pouring herself a cup of coffee. "There's Anna now," Opal said. "I'll bet she's already got an idea of the kind of tenant she wants in the house."

Cora looked up from her phone. "I was telling Opal that the next tenant needs to be a man since Winston left the opening. Otherwise, the balance will be off."

"Preferably handsome and rich," I said to Cora.

"I don't see why either of those attributes would be a problem," Cora said.

"Yes, I'll write that on the advertisement. Must be male, rich and eligible," I said.

"Don't forget handsome," Opal added. "I mean if we're going to go for it, we might as well go all the way."

Tobias was laughing as he headed toward the stairs.

I pulled on my apron. Opal had poured me a cup of coffee. She handed it to me.

"Thanks, I really need this today. I didn't sleep well."

"Why is that?" Opal said. "Is this still about the footsteps I heard on the front porch? Like I said, I was probably just dreaming that."

Cora looked quickly from me to Opal and back to me. "Someone was on the front porch? This is getting scary."

"Did you hear someone, too?" Opal asked.

I turned on the griddle to heat the hashbrowns. I was too exhausted by the subject to rehash all of it. It seemed each of us had had some kind of episode with the stranger, and at the same time, we were no closer to knowing who he was or, for that matter, what he was doing on the island.

"I was sure someone was watching me as I walked home from work yesterday," Cora explained to Opal. I busied myself with breakfast and allowed them to have their own chat. I had nothing much to add in detail or depth to the topic. I'd even seen the man on drone footage and still wouldn't be able to pick him out of a lineup. Naturally, my mind went straight to a police lineup. What if the man was on the island studying our flora and fauna? It wouldn't be the first time a scientist came here to study the plants and animals. Admittedly, the scientists were very open about their reason for the visit, and typically they didn't dress in all dark clothing.

"Well, I was upstairs reading a book. I dozed off but was woken by footsteps on the front porch. No one ever rang the bell or knocked. And Anna said that Olive saw someone out on the trail, a man in dark clothing."

"That's it then," Cora said as she confidently set down her cup of coffee. "That's why we need another man in the house. This island is crawling with weirdos. I think you should add muscular as another requirement on the tenant ad."

I looked pointedly at Opal. She shrugged. "You won't get any arguments from me on that. Maybe a Cary Grant accent, too."

"Yes, an accent." Cora snapped her fingers. "I love the way that posh man talks—the one who played Mr. Darcy—"

"Colin Firth?" I asked. "Maybe we could just ask Mr. Firth to move in. I'm sure he's got plenty of money, and he'd probably love to take a room in our boarding house."

Cora waved her hand dismissively. "Now you're just being silly."

"Yes, I'm the silly one this morning." I scrambled some eggs in a bowl and seasoned them. "Remember, I'm walking you to work today."

"Is that because of there's a killer on the island?" Opal asked. "Guess it wouldn't be the first time." Opal loved to point out that Frostfall seemed to be the destination of choice for murderers. It was true that our lovely island did have more than its share of violent deaths. Thank goodness I'd at least been spared a murder investigation this weekend.

"I think my sister is worried I have a stalker," Cora said blithely as if she hadn't been frightened on her walk home yesterday.

"Well, if you'd rather walk to work alone," I suggested.

"No, it's fine if you want to tag along."

Opal and I exchanged winks.

I poured the eggs onto the sizzling butter and gave them a stir.

"Maybe I should walk with you girls, too," Opal said.

Cora and I looked at her in surprise.

I occasionally managed to talk Opal into a short stroll, especially when she was having problems with insomnia. She spent far too much time watching television and napping, and I worried about her health, but she never liked to venture out far, and the 3Ts was a good distance from the boarding house.

Opal lifted her chin. "I am capable of walking to the 3Ts, you know. I just don't think Anna should walk back on her own, especially not if there's a killer on the loose."

I stirred the eggs again and put down my spoon. "There's no killer on the loose, and I plan to take my bike with me so I can ride back."

Opal's shoulders slumped in relief.

"However, a little exercise," I started.

Opal put up her hand. "I offer my services for protection only. Exercise is not needed. I plan to walk up and down those stairs at least four times today."

I smiled and shook my head. "I suppose that's better than nothing." My phone beeped. I pulled it out of my apron pocket hoping it was Nate. It was a text from the electric company that my payment posted. I still hadn't heard from Nate, and I was working hard not to let it worry me. He couldn't have picked a worse weekend to leave the island.

thirteen

CORA KEPT LOOKING around like a rabbit waiting for a predator. "I'm sorry this has you so tense, Cora. I wouldn't worry about it. There are a lot of people on the island this weekend, and sometimes that's all it takes to ruffle the quiet and make the island feel a little off." I wasn't sure if the pep talk was for my sister or for me. At least the daylight always helped put fears in perspective. The landscape and shrubs and tree shadows didn't seem nearly as menacing this morning.

Cora fussed with a strand of hair that had come untucked from her ponytail. "I'm fine. I just hope it's not as busy at the shop today. I didn't sleep all that well."

In the distance we could see colorful kites hovering and swooping along the shore at the swim beach. "Looks like the kite flyers are out on the beach earlier this morning, so you might get your wish," I said.

We reached the tea shop. I rested my bike against the lamppost. Samuel was outside cleaning off a table. "There you are, Cora. The kite club ordered three dozen strawberry tarts for their evening barbecue, so I'm helping you cover the tables while Sera bakes them. It was busy when we opened. People were lined up waiting for a table, but now, most of them have gone to the beach with their kites."

Cora clapped fast a few times. "Good to hear." She hurried inside to get her apron and start her shift.

"She was exhausted yesterday, and she insists the kite flyers are poor tippers," I said in explanation of her applauding the lack of customers.

"Actually, she's right there. I was out on the floor after I finished in the kitchen. They weren't terribly generous. How is the mountain biking trip?" Samuel winced. "I saw the news about the PTK. How is Nate taking it?" Samuel and Nate had grown close enough that they talked about everything, including Nate's reason for leaving the force.

His questions were a stark reminder that I hadn't heard from Nate yet. "I called him yesterday, but I haven't heard back." It was impossible to hide the worry in my tone. Samuel noticed.

Samuel filled a plastic bin with plates and glasses. "I'm sure he's having too much fun. And after a day on the mountain, all you can do is eat and fall into bed. It's a tough sport."

"I'm sure that's why you guys like it so much. It's challenging and—" I squinted an eye at him. "And I assume it's fun. Although I'm having a hard time understanding that."

"Oh, it's fun all right. Especially the downhill when you're flying down the trail spitting dirt and rocks at the rider behind you. Very satisfying."

I laughed. "I'll have to take your word for it."

Samuel held the bin against one hip and turned toward me. "I don't always catch all the gossip that goes on in the tea shop, but there seemed to be a lot of worry about a strange boat in the harbor. Did we ever find out who it belonged to?"

"No, I'm going to talk to Frannie on my way back to see if she has any news about it." I was talking lightly, but that darn boat had caused me plenty of anguish these past twenty-four hours. "I'll let you get back to work, Sam."

"Say hey to Nate when you talk to him."

"I will." If I ever got to talk to him. I toyed with the idea of sending a text or calling him again, but I decided to wait. What Samuel had said was true. Nate had told me himself that he was always tired after a day mountain biking. After a day on the trails, he usually stopped for a beer and burger with his friends, then he went straight to the motel to shower and fall in bed. If I texted or called again, he might worry that something was wrong, and while everything felt a little off, technically nothing *was* wrong.

The *Salty Bottom* chugged noisily across the harbor. It would be at least five minutes before Frannie docked. I decided to walk along the marina to the end so I could see where the boat had been anchored. Maybe it would be gone, or maybe I'd catch a glimpse of the captain, and he'd be fishing off the side of his boat with a cup of coffee in his hand. All the worries and rumors would be put to rest.

Walking with a bicycle was never ideal, but the weathered

docks made it too rough to ride. I rolled the bike along. The day felt better, lighter, more enjoyable. I planned to stop by the swim beach before heading back to the boarding house. I found the kites calming, and I needed a dose of that.

I reached the final section of marina and stepped past the last tall mast that blocked the view of the harbor. The boat was gone. I did a quick sweep of the water to make sure he hadn't just moved closer to the other boats, but there was no sign of the gray boat. All the tension left my body, and I wanted to scold myself for letting my fear get so out of hand.

I turned back around. The ferry was just reaching the dock. I could see Frannie in her wheelhouse steering the boat in. Passengers were lined up to leave as I reached the ferry. Frannie lowered the gangplank and nodded goodbye to each passenger. There were far fewer people than yesterday. Most of the weekend visitors arrived on Friday.

Fran spotted me and waved. I rested my bike against a railing and walked over to meet her. "The boat is gone," I said excitedly. "But you probably knew that."

Fran smiled. "Gone by the time I reached the marina this morning, thank goodness. Of course, now everyone has shifted their conversations back to the explosive news on the mainland."

"I'm afraid to ask—what explosive news?"

"The Pillow Talk Killer struck again."

It was ridiculous, because having the PTK active again was nothing short of terrifying, but I was relieved that was the explosive news.

"Yes, I've heard."

"He's getting closer," Frannie said in an ominous tone.

"What do you mean?"

"His latest victim was renting a small house right on the beach, just a few hundred yards from the mainland harbor. Of course, everyone is theorizing that the strange boat belonged to the serial killer, and he anchored out here after he killed the poor woman."

"That doesn't make sense. Why would he suddenly be using a boat as his home base? This is the first murder near the harbor. Did he suddenly decide he was a mariner at heart?" I was working hard to disprove everyone's new theory. It was too frightening to consider.

Fran put up her hand. "You don't have to tell me. I think it's a daft notion. Obviously, that boat was here for a stopover. He probably continued up or down the coast. And you're right. There's never been any indication that the PTK was working from the water. Most of the other deaths were inland. It's kind of worrisome though, knowing that he's just a harbor crossing away."

"Well, Cora thinks you should keep a lookout for someone with a shifty eye and evil grin. She's sure you'll be able to spot the infamous killer before he ever reaches our island."

Frannie laughed. I was glad to lighten up the conversation. "I wish I had that ability, and what's a shifty eye, anyhow?"

"I have no idea, but hopefully, you'll know it when you see

it. I'm just glad that boat is gone. I think I'll head over to the swim beach and watch the kites before I go back home for chores."

"Have a good day," Fran called as I climbed on my bike and pedaled away.

My phone rang as I reached the beach. I pulled it out and practically cheered. It was Nate. "Hello," I tried not to sound anxious, but I wasn't sure it worked.

"Hey, is everything all right?" he asked. (Obviously it hadn't worked.)

"Everything is fine. How are you doing?" I asked tentatively.

"Good. I just fixed a rim. Hit a rock on the way down. And it's a little windy right now, so I'm holding off for a bit while I eat some snacks."

"That's good, only I wasn't asking so much about your riding adventure as—" I ended it there.

"Oh, you mean the news. Yeah, it hit me pretty hard. That's why I didn't call you last night. I was a little drunk. I bought myself a six-pack and wallowed in self-pity in my dingy motel room. But the sun came up and the mountain trails beckoned, so I'm feeling better now. Whatever happened to that boat in the marina?" he asked.

"Gone," I said happily. "We must have been a brief pitstop. I just got to the beach to watch the kites. I'm glad you're having a good time."

"Yep, having a great time. I'll be back tomorrow morning. Have fun kite-watching."

"See you tomorrow. Love you." I hung up. The morning was going just as I hoped. The mystery boat was gone without incident, and despite what had happened in the news, Nate was having a good time. Now it was time to admire the kites.

fourteen

AARON WRIGHT'S dragon kite was conspicuously absent from the blue sky, but there were plenty of other wonderful kites to fill the air space. I glanced around but didn't see Aaron at all. He was probably too disappointed in the loss of his dragon to return to the beach. It was a shame, and there was really only one person to blame. And that person was enjoying all the attention now with his fighter jet kite. The young kids on the beach pointed at the big jet-shaped kite as it swooped and dove and shot higher in the air.

"That is an impressive kite," a voice said next to me.

I glanced over. It was Dirk.

"Oh, hello, where's your buzzy friend?" I asked.

"He's out of fuel. I'm charging him for later."

We both turned our attention back to the kites. A man wearing a bright yellow cap lifted a giant shark kite into the air. Its tail waved back and forth like a real shark as it *swam* higher into the air. Its jaw was massive with big white teeth jutting out from a wide grin.

"I don't think I saw that one yesterday," I said.

"He arrived late in the afternoon. I met him when he took his kite out for a test flight after everyone else had gone in for the day. His name is Wesley Campbell. I like that kite. It's giving the jet fighter a run for its money," Dirk pointed out.

He was right. Many of the young spectators ran in the direction of the shark. "The poor fighter jet just can't compete with the monsters of nature," I said. "First, the dragon, and now, a shark."

I watched as the man with the shark deftly coaxed the kite higher in the sky. He was wearing a camouflage t-shirt and cargo shorts along with the bright yellow cap. He was a big, burly sort, maybe early fifties, and nothing about him said "kite flyer." He looked more suited to be sitting at the helm of a cargo ship or an army helicopter.

Owen had his scarlet parrot in the sky. Sadie was sitting nearby on a beach chair reading a book. It seemed she'd had enough of the kite show. I looked around the crowd for Lyla and found her standing under a wide-brimmed hat near the lemonade kiosk. She was taking pictures of the kites.

"Did you catch anything else interesting on your drone?" I asked.

"Not after we spoke, but it was an interesting afternoon," Dirk said cryptically.

I didn't know either of the couples personally, so I took the liberty to ask. "Did you happen to catch a pair of kite club members in an embrace?"

Dirk blushed again. "You could say that."

I turned more toward him. "It seems you don't even need a drone for spying. I happened upon the club president, Theo Martin, in the middle of some heavy flirting. Only it wasn't with Lyla, his girlfriend."

Dirk nodded shyly. "Yeah, that's what I saw, too. I hadn't meant to catch them on tape, but they were hiding behind some shrubs, and I happened to fly the drone that direction."

"Couldn't be helped, I'm sure. I was riding my bike back home, and after seeing your footage of the man in the black hat, I was staying vigilant. I spotted Theo and Sadie on the bridge near my house."

"What happened with that man? Has anyone found out who he was?" Dirk asked. "I looked closer at the footage, but there was no way to see his face. I definitely got the impression that he was running out of sight of the drone."

"I think you're right. I don't know for certain, but I think he's left the island and the harbor." I realized as I said it that I never made a full connection between the boat and the stranger. What if there was no connection? Was the stranger still on the island? I pushed that unsettling thought out of my mind.

A commotion on the sand pulled our attention back to the kites. The source of the commotion became instantly apparent. The massive shark had gotten itself tangled up with Theo's fighter jet.

"I was wondering when this would happen," I said. "There are so many kites out here and only so much airspace above the swim beach."

Dirk shook his head. "And me without my drone. It's hard to tell who's at fault, but both men look angry."

Dirk was right. The owner of the shark kite, Wesley, had a red face beneath his bright yellow cap. Both kites nosedived into the sand. Wesley threw down his spool and marched toward Theo. Everyone watched with great interest as the two men came toe-to-toe. The kites laid in a crumpled heap on the wet sand.

"You did that on purpose," Wesley yelled.

"That was entirely your fault," Theo yelled back.

I glanced toward Lyla. She was holding onto her hat and watching the scene on the sand, but she made no attempt to step into the fray. Sadie looked almost as uninterested as Lyla.

"You were trying to sabotage my kite just like you did to Aaron's dragon kite. I heard all about it yesterday—how you purposely stepped on it."

"That numbskull left his kite in the middle of the sand. I was backing up and didn't see it," Theo insisted.

Dirk and I had witnessed the whole thing. He shot me a sideways glance. "I think we both know that's not true," he muttered.

"I agree."

"You have no right being president of this club. You're a petty, jealous toddler," Wesley snapped.

It was too much for Theo. He lunged forward and shoved Wesley hard. Wesley was a big man, but he took two faltering steps backward. Some of the other club members had reeled their kites in, and a few were headed toward the argument.

"Come on, gentlemen, this is no way to behave," a man said. He waved his hand toward the group of curious, young onlookers. "Let's model better behavior." The man was sounding far too reasonable, and the two men in the center of the fight weren't ready for reason.

Theo lunged toward Wesley, but Wesley managed to step clear of him.

"My money's on the big man in the yellow hat," Dirk joked.

After missing Wesley entirely, Theo stumbled forward a few steps, caught himself, twirled around and pulled back his arm. His fist grazed Wesley's jaw enough to send Wesley back a few more steps.

"Huh, guess I put my money on the wrong man," Dirk said.

"I wouldn't be too sure." I motioned their direction.

Wesley regained his balance and lunged at Theo. Theo emerged holding a bloody nose.

"Well, this is getting gory," I commented.

"Yup, and me without my drone," Dirk complained again.

I hoped some of the other members would step in before more blood was shed. Wesley regrouped. His big fists were rounded as he stepped toward Theo. Three men jumped in to stop the fight. Two held back Wesley and one pulled at Theo's arm to keep him from taking a swing while Wesley was restrained.

Wesley yanked free of the men holding him. His hat flew

off as he marched toward his kite. If he was hoping for a fast, dramatic exit, it didn't happen. It took Wesley a few minutes to free his shark from the jet. One of the kids ran over to hand him back his yellow cap. He pulled it down on his head and marched off the beach. Theo walked dejectedly toward his jet kite. It was limp and broken. He picked it up and glanced around the beach. It would make sense that he was looking for Lyla, his girlfriend, but his gaze stopped when it landed on Sadie. She smiled demurely at him, but that was her only response. Was he showing off in front of her? It was starting to look that way. In the meantime, I wasn't the only person to notice their subtle interaction. Lyla's pretty smile had turned to an angry frown. Like Wesley, she marched angrily off the beach…but without a shark in tow.

fifteen

I SPENT the rest of the morning puttering around the house. I felt much better now that the boat was gone, and my world seemed to be back the way I liked it. I was cleaning out Huck's water bowl when Opal joined me in the kitchen.

"I'm having a craving for potato salad," she said as she sat down. "My mom used to make a big tub of it for our end of summer picnic. She always added in sweet pickle chips. They were my favorite part."

I filled Huck's bowl with fresh water and walked it across to his food tray. "I haven't made potato salad at all this summer. You know what—you've got me craving it, too. I have some sweet pickles in the fridge." I walked to the pantry and looked inside. "I hope you still feel strongly about those sweet pickles because they'll be the main ingredient. I'm out of potatoes."

Opal's posture slumped. "I don't suppose you can make potato salad without the star ingredient."

I pulled out my phone. "I'll text Molly. She always stays open late on the weekend." I sent off a text asking about her potato inventory. She wrote right back that she still had a basket full of yellow potatoes. I texted that I was on my way. "Success," I told Opal. I'm heading out to buy potatoes."

"Yum, and celery," Opal added with a nostalgic sparkle in her eye. "Mom always put in chopped celery."

I nodded. "Celery is a must."

I decided to make quick work of my potato excursion, so I pulled out my bike and rode down to the harbor. The kite club had shut down the exhibition early to set up for their end-of-event barbecue down on the beach. They'd had great weather all morning, but the wind had picked up now, and the occasional strong gust whipped up from the shore. Molly was adjusting her big umbrella as I reached the produce stand.

She looked over her shoulder when my bike brakes squeaked. "Anna, it's you." She tugged and turned the umbrella so that it wasn't taking the brunt of the onshore wind. "There, now you stay put, you big nuisance," she scolded the umbrella. "I wasn't expecting these gale force winds this afternoon. I'm going to shut down early before it gets worse." Right then, a shot of wind pushed the umbrella. It flapped and spun slightly but held its place.

"It's picked up a lot since this morning." I pulled out my canvas shopping bag and began to fill it with firm yellow potatoes.

"Potato soup?" Molly asked. "I guess it's too hot for soup."

"Opal was having a fond moment of nostalgia about summer picnics and her mom's potato salad."

"Ah, potato salad. Of course. Perfect for the end of summer."

Two people with kite t-shirts came up to the stand. "Oh look, Mike," the woman said. "There are some nice lemons. We can make lemonade."

The man, Mike, was just ending a phone call. He shook his head. "They still can't find Theo. No one has seen him since his kite tangled with Wes's."

The woman clucked her tongue as she picked out some lemons. "Knowing Theo, he's off sulking somewhere. After this event, we really need to have a new election."

Mike shrugged. "No one wants the position. Way too much work and very little reward."

"I'm sure he'll show up," the woman said.

"He's supposed to be helping us set up the grill," Mike complained.

The woman paid for the lemons, and the couple walked away. "That was interesting," Molly said. "Why would a grown man be sulking?" she asked.

"I can answer that. His fighter jet kite got ruined when it tangled itself with a shark kite."

Molly laughed. "Forget I asked." Another sharp breeze reminded her it was time to shut down for the day. I paid for the potatoes, dropped the bag into the basket on my bike and said goodbye to Molly.

I rode along the path and spotted Dirk sitting on a bench

eating an ice cream. His loyal buddy, the drone, was sitting next to him. He waved for me to stop.

I pulled over to the bench.

"I see your drone has refueled." I looked pointedly at the device.

He patted it gently. "Did you hear?" Dirk asked. "Rumor has it Theo stomped off with his kite and was never seen again. He's in charge of the barbecue this afternoon, but he's not answering his phone. People think he's pouting about the broken kite. I guess kite flying keeps you stuck in childhood no matter what your age."

"I'd say that Theo might lose his presidential status after this year's event. Enjoying the ice cream? Let me guess—butter pecan? It's one of my favorites."

Dirk held up the half-eaten cone. "Best I've had in a long time."

"Are you staying much longer?" I asked.

"Through tomorrow. I want to get some overhead shots of the lighthouses."

"That'll be nice. They've been recently renovated, so I'm sure they'll make good models. Have a good rest of the day."

"Thanks, I'm off to go through some of the footage I got in the last few hours."

I took off again and headed toward the trail. Halfway home, I spotted a group of ravens chattering, squawking and hovering over the river. Something must have died near the water. I left the bike on the side of the trail and headed in the direction of the ravens in case it was a duck or goose that needed help. If it was sick or hurt, I could take it to the rescue. The ravens would have to look elsewhere for their next meal.

As I neared the spot they were so handily pointing out with their loud caws, I noticed that the river current was rushing around something large. The ravens begrudgingly flew up to the surrounding trees to watch. They weren't ready to let the meal go yet.

I pushed back some of the shrubby growth above the riverbank and stepped through it. I gasped when I saw what had held the ravens' interest. A man was floating face down in the river. His shirt had caught on a submerged tree root, so he bobbed in place between a boulder and the bank. His limbs weren't moving at all.

I raced to water's edge and stepped into ice-cold, shin-deep water. I scrambled to unhook his shirt from the tree limb. There was no sign of life. The water kept him buoyant enough that I was able to easily pull him closer to shore. I had to trudge deeper into the fast-running current to turn him onto his back. I crouched down and used all my strength to flip him over. It was Theo Martin. There was a tennis-ball-sized bump the side of his head, and his lips were blue with death.

I climbed on the bank, clear of the rushing water. The ravens gave up and flew off to look for something else to eat. Theo was a big man, and his feet were still in the water. I took hold of his limp arm and gave it a sharp pull. His body budged but only slightly. The mud on the banks was like glue. I pulled once more and only succeeded in landing on my bottom. Sitting down next to Theo's body, I discovered another grisly detail. A long strand of nylon string was tied tightly around his throat. It cut into his skin, leaving a red mark around his neck. At first, I'd allowed myself to believe that this was a terrible accident, that Theo had slipped on a rock in the river and smacked his head before drowning. But this was no accident. Someone strangled Theo Martin with kite string.

I pulled out my phone to call the police on the mainland. They'd send Detective Norwich out to investigate the death. Norwich was a rude, arrogant and completely incompetent detective, which was why a murder case on the island always fell to me. I had no experience in law enforcement, but somehow, I'd been put in charge of island mishaps, and this was definitely a mishap. The kite string around the victim's neck would make it next to impossible for Norwich to pull his usual shenanigans and close this as an accident. Although, I never put it past the man. He was truly an imbecile.

I stared down at the limp body. His eyes were slightly open, and his bluish, droopy mouth had sand trickling out of it. A dead body was always a shocking sight. And here I thought the weekend had improved.

sixteen

I'D MADE the call to the police, but it would be at least an hour before Norwich arrived on the island. Frannie would be called to pick him up, and he was never in a hurry to get here. It angered him that our small island was part of his jurisdiction, and it especially enraged him that I was constantly correctly solving the cases that he messed up. Detective Norwich disliked me immensely, and I would make myself scarce as soon as he arrived. In the meantime, I had a chance to do some investigating on my own. I was already ahead of Norwich because I'd witnessed two altercations Theo had with other club members. And then there was his secret tryst with Owen's fiancée, Sadie. Had Owen discovered their affair? It seemed Lyla knew all about it. She'd argued with Theo outside of the tea shop, and there were accusations of cheating being tossed around. The list of possible suspects was long. Briefly, I considered that the mystery man in the black cap had been involved, but I had no reason to believe he was still on the island. At least I hoped that was the case.

It was impossible for me to move Theo higher on the shore, but I had him solidly on land and out of the stronger current. I took a few photos of Theo. The water splashed against the bottom of his shoes and then crested over the tops of his feet. With some effort, I pulled one leg free of the current and took a picture of the thick tread on Theo's shoe. If I found footprints, I'd need to know which ones belonged to Theo and which ones were left behind by the killer.

I surveyed the patch of area I was standing in. There was no sign of broken shrubs or something heavy being dragged across the bank. I had to move the shrubs aside just to reach the water. If Theo had been killed on land and then dragged to the river, I would see, at the very least, a disturbance in the mud along the bank. The only footprints were the ones I left behind as I raced toward the water. Had Theo been killed upstream? His shirt was caught on a submerged tree root, otherwise he might very well have drifted downstream and all the way to where Moon River empties into the sea. That might have been the killer's intention, only the submerged root grabbed hold of the body on its way downstream.

I hiked upstream, parallel with the river, taking care to keep off the muddy parts of the bank. There were still a lot of questions about how Theo died. Did the killer knock him out, strangle him and then push him in the river? Had the killer snuck up behind Theo, strangled him and then pushed him into the river where he hit his head on a rock? Had Theo drowned during the attack? None of the questions would be properly answered without a coroner's autopsy.

Unfortunately, my status as amateur sleuth did not give me access to official reports. I was on my own to solve this because I knew for certain the detective with the privilege of all the official reports was never going to find the killer. If Norwich wasn't able to label the death an accident, then he usually resorted to his next lazy move—arresting the first person he met with a possible motive. He never had anything to back up his arrests, and they always ended with some poor soul having to suffer the humiliation and terror of an arrest for a crime they didn't commit.

It wasn't easy to stay parallel with the water. Occasionally trees or shrubs turned my path away from the water and up to the trail, but I meandered along, determined to find the exact location of the murder.

The onshore wind kicked up enough energy that the trees shook their branches overhead. My shoes sloshed with river water. I sat on a broken tree trunk to take off my shoes and wring out my socks. There was nothing more irritating than walking in wet shoes. As I pulled off my first shoe, something tickled the ankle of the foot that was still on the ground. I startled and pulled both knees up, planting my feet on the tree trunk. I leaned down expecting to see a large spider or insect. Instead, a shiny piece of silver paper wriggled in the wind. It was jammed far enough beneath the trunk that the wind hadn't carried it away. I pulled it free and examined it. I'd seen silver strips just like it tied to the tail of Aaron Wright's dragon kite. The tail piece was light and obviously prone to being airborne, but it would have had to catch the right current of wind to make it all the way to the river from the swim beach. Still, it was possible.

I stuck the silver ribbon in my pocket and finished wringing out my socks. I decided to push those into my pockets as well. There was no sense pulling wet socks back on. I got up, dusted myself off and took my first step to continue my mission. That was when I noticed that the large cinnamon fern growing a few feet up from the river had been trampled. It was flattened in the middle, and several of the ferny fronds had been ripped free of the plant.

I walked closer to the water, making sure not to disturb any prints. I found no clear footprints, which was aggravating considering the mud would have been the perfect medium for a clear cast. However, the mud along the bank had been disturbed by something, and my guess would be that it was from multiple footprints. And from the look of the smeared mess in the mud, there had been a struggle. It led me to believe that the killer had snuck up on Theo, wrapped kite string around his neck and then Theo fought for his life as the string cut off his airway.

Had Theo traipsed into the landscape to meet up with Sadie? Was he just out for a walk? Had someone lured him to the river so they could kill him and send his body downriver to the ocean? There were so many questions to answer. I needed to pull out my corkboards and fill out cards for the many suspects that were lining up in my head.

It seemed I'd found the place where Theo was killed. I took photos of the trampled fern and the mud. I searched farther upstream for more evidence. And I found it. Another question was answered. A small clearing with soil that was wet from being so close to the river showed several large, man-sized footprints. I pulled out my phone and scrolled to the photo of Theo's shoe tread. It matched the prints in the clearing. There were other footprints, much smaller and with less tread, like the smooth bottom of a sandal. In several spots the sandals and Theo's shoes were facing each other and very close. This had been Theo and Sadie's latest secret meeting place. Had Owen discovered them and lost his temper? But where did the kite string come from? This murder seemed planned. However, was it so farfetched to think that a kite enthusiast might be walking around with a spool of kite string in their pocket? If only Dirk had had his drone up and running, I might have made quick work of this case.

Further survey of the area showed several more plants that had been broken but no clear footprints other than the ones left behind by Theo and Sadie in the clearing. I was slowly piecing the whole scene together in my head, but there were still too many possible versions to give me a clear picture.

My phone beeped. I pulled it out of my pocket. It was from Fran. "I've just landed on the mainland, and the gross toothpick-chewer is waiting to come on board." Along with having a terrible disposition, Detective Norwich had a disgusting habit of constantly chewing on a toothpick. "What's going on?" Fran asked.

"Seems as if the strange weekend just got weirder. There's

been a murder. Let Norwich know that I'll be waiting on the west side of Calico Trail, near the bend in the river."

"Will do. And sorry about this, Anna. I'm sure it's the last thing you wanted. It's not anyone we know, is it?"

"One of the kite club members, and a prominent one at that." While my phone was out, I took a few more photos of the clearing and the broken plants. Then I headed back to the path to find my bike.

Opal would have to wait a little longer for her potato salad.

seventeen

I WAS sure it was mostly in my head, but I could always smell a faint stench in the air whenever Norwich had stepped on the island. Fran's directions probably confused the man, so I waited out on the trail for him. Today, he had a young, inexperienced-looking uniformed officer with him. The poor man probably got stuck accompanying Norwich because of low seniority. It was never an easy job being Norwich's assistant.

Norwich usually wore a rumpled old coat, but today, he'd left the grimy garment behind because of the summer weather. I wished he'd done the same with the toothpick, but it jutted from his thin lips like always. His expression turned extra snarky when he spotted me.

My whole body tightened at the sight of his arrogant smirk. "St. James, it figures you'd be here."

"I knew you'd be anxious to see the crime scene, as

usual." The sarcasm was thick whenever Norwich was around.

The young officer had gotten windburned on the ferry ride. His cheeks were red. His eyes rounded at my comment.

"Sure, sure." Norwich looked at his assistant. "Officer Perkins, this is the island busybody who likes to pretend she's a homicide detective."

The officer dipped his head coyly. "It's Harper," he muttered.

Norwich's toothpick moved up and down like a lever. "Eh? Speak up, kid."

The officer lifted his chin. It seemed he was so young he was still learning how to use a razor. There were tiny nicks on his clean-shaven throat. "It's Officer Harper, sir. Not Perkins."

I turned my head to hide my smile.

Norwich ignored the correction. "We've got it from here, St. James. Go home."

"Oh, you've got it, do you? Then, off you go," I said and waved my hand toward the thick landscape separating the trail from the river. I was a good fifteen yards up the trail from where I'd found Theo's body.

Norwich scowled at the shrubs and trees. "Why don't you people do some yardwork on this island? How am I supposed to work in all that?" He looked around. "Who found the body? That's the person I need to see. Not you."

I crossed my arms and smiled. "You're looking at that person, but you're right, I should head home." I turned to leave.

"Not so fast, St. James."

I turned back toward him. "Yes? What is it?"

"Well, don't just stand there," Norwich barked. "Show us where the body is, and, on the way, you can explain to me how you just happened upon yet another dead body on this island."

I shrugged. "It was really quite easy. The ravens had started gathering for their next meal." I regretted being so flippant about it because my comment caused some of the windburn on Officer Harper's cheeks to fade. I started off and moved at a pace I knew would be hard for the out-of-shape detective. He also hated things like walking through shrubs and mud, so I made sure to take the worst possible path to the river. My devious plan worked. He muttered cuss words and groaned angrily all the way to the water.

We reached the bank. Officer Harper had taken to holding back some of the shrubs and tree limbs so Norwich could get through without trouble. Norwich reminded me of spoiled royalty as he stepped past the restrained branches without so much as a thank-you to his assistant.

I stopped short, not wanting to get too close to the body. Norwich would have a temper tantrum about me messing up the crime scene. Norwich stopped short, too, when he noticed that the ground had started to turn to mud. He glanced down at his leather loafers and then toward the body. "Looks like he fell in the river and drowned. Clearly an accident."

Norwich was always lazy about these cases, but this time he was really pushing the limit.

I cleared my throat. "Maybe you should get closer. I think you'll—

Norwich rudely put his stubby hand in my face. "I don't need to know what you think."

In the meantime, Officer Harper had trekked through the mud to get a better look at the body. He crouched down next to Theo.

"Detective Norwich, sir, I think you should come look at this."

I smiled sweetly at Norwich to let him know he was once again wrong.

Norwich grumbled the entire way to the bank of the river. One particular step took his nice leather loafer deep into the mud. It stuck there until he gave his leg a sharp tug. The sudden movement nearly caused Norwich to fall sideways, but he managed to right himself.

"Darn it," I muttered under my breath. It would have made my day to see him land in the mud.

"That lump on his head tells me he slipped and hit it on a rock. Probably drowned," Norwich said confidently.

Harper had to point out the string around Theo's neck. Norwich grew quiet. He pulled out some glasses and gave it a closer look. Then he looked back at me. "You didn't tie that there to make this look like a murder, did you?"

My chin dropped, and I had no words. Norwich had said a lot of awful things to me, but this accusation was one too far.

"Detective Norwich, you are the single worst detective in the world, and I don't need to meet all of them first to make that assessment. There can't be anyone worse. There just can't be. Of course I didn't tie that string around his neck. Someone strangled him and pushed his body into the river hoping he'd float out to sea. And if you can stop with the baseless accusations, I can tell you exactly where I found him—"

His face reddened as he straightened. Admittedly, I might have pushed it too far with my earlier comment about him being the world's worst detective and especially in front of his young partner, but he deserved it. "So, what you're telling me is that you already messed up this entire crime scene."

To think I could have been home in my wonderful kitchen sipping iced tea and chopping potatoes. Next time, I'd ignore the ravens. I took a deep breath. I needed to be the reasonable person in this scuffle.

"I spotted a group of ravens hovering over the river," I said calmly. "I walked toward them to see if an injured animal needed help, and I found Mr. Martin floating face down in the river. His shirt had gotten stuck on a submerged tree root. Being a normal and caring human—" I said to him pointedly (there was no need to be overly polite) "—I jumped into the water to turn him face up and get him out of the current in case he was still alive."

The officer absently nodded along with my explanation. He knew it was the right thing to do, but Norwich wasn't convinced.

"Did you at least take a picture so we could see where he was before you disturbed the crime scene?" Norwich asked.

"I guess you didn't hear the part about me wanting to get

him out of the current in case he was still alive. Stopping for pictures would hardly have helped if he needed resuscitation."

Officer Harper seemed to realize this was not how a murder investigation should proceed. He pulled out a notepad. "You said the man's name was Martin, Miss—" he paused for me to fill in the name, but Norwich did it for him.

"St. James, Nosy St. James," Norwich snarled.

"Anna St. James," I corrected calmly. The man had gotten my ire up, but I decided not to stoop to his level. "That's right. His name is Theo Martin. He's here on the island with the National Kite Club. They're here for the weekend. Earlier some of the club members were looking for him. Theo Martin is the president of the club."

"See, what did I tell you about her being nosy?" Norwich muttered over his toothpick.

The officer ignored him. "Is there anything else you can tell us about the victim, Miss St. James?"

I had plenty, but I wasn't about to help Norwich with details. Not that he'd listen to them anyhow. "You'll want to talk to the club members to learn more about him," I said. "Most are staying at the hotel. He's here with a girlfriend, too. No one knows about his death yet. And one last thing before I leave."

Norwich waved angrily at me. "You've been enough help." He rolled his eyes. "We won't be able to find footprints since you've traipsed all around the crime scene." An evil grin appeared. "Or maybe we'll just take *you* in for questioning."

"And that's my cue to leave." I smiled politely at Officer Harper. He looked aggravated as he nodded his thank-you to me. I hiked back through the shrubs and trees and climbed on my bike. It was time to set up those corkboards.

eighteen

OPAL HAD BEEN LOOKING SO FORWARD to the potato salad, I decided I could multitask and make the salad while filling out the cards for my corkboard. Tobias was bored, so he joined me for both tasks. I set him up with his own cutting board and knife for the celery and red onion. I finished chopping the potatoes, dropped them into a pot of water and turned the burner on.

Opal came downstairs to join us. "Oh, the corkboards are out. Who died?" She poured herself a glass of iced tea and sat down at the table. "Are those the potatoes for the salad?" she asked before her first question could be answered.

"They sure are. I was hoping to be farther along with the salad, but I got sidetracked by a murder."

Opal sighed. "Most people would find that statement shocking, but it's not the case on Frostfall Island. Who got killed this time?"

"The president of the kite club," Tobias replied. "Anna

found him because the ravens were getting ready to have him as a meal."

"Crudely put, but true. I think the killer was trying to send him down the river to the ocean, but a jutting tree root stopped his progress. If not for the ravens, Theo Martin might have been floating there for a long time."

"Or at least as long as it took the ravens to do their work," Tobias said.

Opal looked over at him with a crooked smile. "Someone is full of vinegar this afternoon."

Tobias blushed and he put down the knife. "I'm sorry, you're right. That's not like me." He wiped his eye.

"Well, you don't have to cry about it," Opal said. "We all get that way every once in a while."

Tobias looked at her confused, then nodded. "Oh, the tears. That's from the onion. I'm not crying."

I walked over with a bowl and swept the pile of red onions off the cutting board. "Nice work on the onion. Perfect little squares," I told Tobias with a wink. He still looked ashamed about what he'd said earlier.

"I'll start on the celery next," he said with a renewed smile. "What have you got for the corkboards? I'm interested to hear."

I took off my apron and pulled on my investigator hat, metaphorically speaking. I wrote down Theo Martin on a card and stuck it in the middle of the board. "Theo Martin's body was discovered, by yours truly, floating face down in the river about a hundred yards from the bridge. He had a large bump on his head. A piece of nylon string, kite string, I presume, was tied tightly around his neck."

Tobias sat up straighter. "Was he strangled. Or was he drowned?"

"Or was it the smack to his noggin?" Opal added.

"All good questions and ones I've been trying to answer myself. My working theory is that Theo had gone into the trees to meet up with the woman he was having a secret affair with. Someone followed him, came up from behind and wrapped the string around his neck. There was a struggle, but Theo eventually ran out of air. The killer pushed him into the river where he smacked his head. His body was then carried away by the strong current, and his journey to the sea was halted by the jutting tree root."

"A secret affair?" Opal said with a twinkle in her eye. "Sounds like we've got a scandal and crime of passion. Was it the betrayed lover?"

"It might have been." I grabbed another card and started writing. "His name is Owen Perez, and he's engaged to a woman named Sadie Moore." I wrote each name on a card and jotted down a few notes. "Sadie has been secretly seeing Theo Martin, the victim. I spotted them together on the bridge yesterday. That brings me to Theo's girlfriend, Lyla Rogers. Theo and Lyla had a very public spat about his cheating in front of the 3Ts yesterday morning." I wrote down Lyla's name adding jealous girlfriend to the description.

"Who knew there could be so much intrigue in a kite club," Opal mused. "But it sounds like your case is going to be easy. Obviously, Owen did it."

Tobias's face popped up. He'd been listening while cutting celery. "Why not the girlfriend, Lyla?"

"Well, it's usually the man," Opal said. She had had her own intrigue earlier in life when her then-husband cheated on her.

"I think Tobias is right. We can't cross Lyla off the list either. I'm hoping to talk to some of these people to find out where they were this afternoon. I saw Theo this morning on the swim beach, and he was very much alive, so I can estimate his time of death somewhere between noon and an hour ago when I spotted him in the river. It should be easy enough to find out where everyone was. And that brings me to another suspect."

I pulled out a new color of index card and wrote down Wesley Campbell. I drew a quick sketch of a shark to remind me that he was the man with the shark kite. There were enough unfamiliar names going on the board that I needed little drawings to keep them separate.

"Will this be enough celery?" Tobias piled up the celery on the board.

I looked at Opal for approval. "That looks about right."

"Thanks for helping with that, Toby." I left my corkboards to collect the celery in the same bowl as the onions. "I got way behind after finding the body. I had to wait for Norwich—"

Tobias and Opal both groaned at the name. "I thought the whole vibe on the island had gotten darker," Opal said. "That explains it."

Tobias laughed. "So, what did Norwich have to say? Was

he already planning to make an arrest?" All my housemates—in fact, all the island locals—knew what a disaster Norwich was in a homicide investigation.

"He was trying to insinuate that I staged the whole thing to make it look like a murder instead of an accident." I'd forgotten about his out-of-line comment at the river, but now it came back like a slap in the face. It was by far the worst thing he'd ever said to me, and he'd said plenty of horrible things.

Tobias's mouth dropped open. "You've got to be kidding me!"

"I wish I was."

Opal clucked her tongue in disgust. "Isn't there some formal complaint you can make to his captain? It seems there should be punishment for such an offensive accusation."

"Nate says Norwich has connections to the chief of police, a relative or something, and that has shielded him all these years. Anyone else would have been fired for incompetency."

"Nepotism," Tobias said angrily. "Nothing worse. So, what about that next card? We need to solve this before that imbecile arrests our Anna."

Opal sat up in agreement. "Yes, tell us about that green card in your hand."

"This is for Wesley Campbell. He brought out a magnificent shark kite this morning. It wasn't in the air long before the shark got tangled up with Theo Martin's fighter jet kite. It was hard to tell how it all happened, but the two men acted like angry boys in the schoolyard. Name calling, shoving and a fist or two. A few of the other people on the beach stepped in before it got nasty."

Tobias carried the knife and cutting board to the sink. "Hardly seems fair that Wesley blamed Theo for the kite fiasco."

"Yes, except there was an incident yesterday, the first day of the kite fair, and in that fiasco, it seemed Theo *was* to blame." I wrote down the name Aaron Wright on a yellow card and drew a dragon in the corner. "A man named Aaron Wright carried a beautiful dragon kite out to the beach."

"Yes, I saw that one. Very impressive," Tobias said as he sat back down.

"Well, it was the hit of the beach. All the spectators were admiring it, but while Aaron took a break, he had it resting in the sand. Theo backed up and stepped on it. It broke in half. The whole thing looked contrived from where I stood. Aaron thought so, too. He yelled at Theo and left the beach very upset." I reached into the pocket of my shorts and pulled out the silver strip of metallic paper. "This is the kind of paper Aaron was using on the tail of his kite. I found this near the place that I think Theo was murdered."

"Sounds like a major piece of evidence," Tobias noted.

"You could be right." I added a note about it to the card and pinned the card to the board.

"Looks like you've got your work cut out for you," Opal said as we all stared at the colorful board.

"Yep, you know it's a big one when I run out of colors in the index card deck."

nineteen

A LARGE BOWL of potato salad was chilling in the refrigerator. Opal was my official taste tester, and she told me it was as good as her mom's, which I considered a great compliment. The days were still long, and the sun had only started to dip in the sky. The earlier wind had settled to a calm breeze as I left the house for my investigation.

"What a day. Actually, what a weekend," Frannie texted as I reached the west side of Chicory Trail.

I was about to write back but decided that kind of open-ended text required a phone call. I dialed Fran and was pleased when she picked up.

"So, you're not on the water," I said instead of the usual hello.

"No, I'm at the dock. The Coast Guard just dropped off the coroner and his team. They should be heading your way soon."

In the distance I spotted four people with a gurney and some equipment. This wasn't going to be the easiest body removal. "I see them. I guess Norwich is still down at the river." It was unlike him to spend so much time at a crime scene. He liked to leave the dirty work to everyone else. (I was part of that group.)

"No, I saw Norwich on the wharf gobbling an ice cream. If you're wondering if he eats ice cream around that darn toothpick—yes, yes, he does, and it's not a pleasant sight."

"There goes my surprise about him spending so much time at the crime scene. I wonder if he's even told the kite club about Theo's death."

"I assume so because he's apparently asked the club members to stay on the island." Frannie pulled the phone away temporarily. "If you're with the kite club, then I can't take you across until I get word from the detective." She returned to our call. "They are not happy, and now I have to be the grumpy gatekeeper in all of this."

"Well, at least Norwich did one thing right so far. It would be impossible to solve this if everyone left the island. It's a national club, so I assume people came here from all over the country. I'm sorry that you've got the unenviable position of reminding people they're stuck on the island."

"By the way, I think most of the kite club members are gathering down on the swim beach. They've decided to fly their kites as a tribute to their late president," Fran said.

"Oh, perfect, then all my suspects will be in one place. I'm heading that way now. Do you see Norwich anywhere in the vicinity? I want to avoid him."

"Gee, I can't imagine why," she teased. "Let me see." She

stopped, and I heard her sniffing through the phone. "Don't smell him, so he's not nearby."

I laughed. "It seems we all have the exact same opinion of the man, and I have to say, for me, this encounter with him has to be the worst of all. I'll talk to you later, Fran."

I picked up my pace. If there was an impromptu memorial at the beach, then I needed to be there. It was the perfect opportunity to talk to each of my suspects and see how they were feeling about the news. It was always better to get their first reaction when they heard the news but then that privilege was mostly afforded to the officials. I usually had to sweep in after the fact.

I could see kites taking flight in the distance. Sera popped her head out of the tea shop when she saw me hurrying past. The shop was near closing, and the place was empty. Cora was cleaning off tables. "Hey, I've heard there's been a murder," Sera said.

Cora looked up from her task. "Again? It's those kite people, isn't it? Poor tippers," she muttered as if murder and tipping badly had a scientifically-based connection.

"I've got dozens of strawberry tarts waiting for a barbecue that isn't going to happen."

Sera stepped out and walked over to me. "Someone said it was the club president. I had a few people come into the shop earlier to look for him, but I hadn't seen him all day. Wasn't there an incident with his girlfriend?" she asked.

"Yes, I'm going to the beach now to see what I can learn from the other members."

"I won't keep you then. Wait, does that mean *he's* on the island?"

"Norwich? Yep, he's slithering about somewhere. I'm trying to avoid him. See you later." I was anxious to get to the beach.

"Keep me posted," Sera called. I waved back at her.

The beautiful dragon kite took flight in the blue sky as I reached the beach. Aaron looked pleased to have his dragon airborne again. I decided to walk straight over to him. Aaron had fair skin, and it seemed he'd been less than thorough with his sunblock. Patches of red were developing on his arms and his forehead. Colorful kites danced in the breeze, but the whole event looked decidedly somber.

Aaron smiled up at his kite as it swooped through the air. "It's wonderful to see your dragon in the sky again," I said.

He pulled his gaze from the kite and looked over his shoulder. "Thank you."

I stopped next to him. "I was here when Theo Martin accidently stepped on your kite yesterday."

"Yes." The quickest eyeroll followed. One thing was certain, Aaron didn't look terribly distraught about the shocking news. "I wasn't sure I'd get him patched up. The damage was severe."

I moved a little closer. "Forgive me for saying this, but it almost looked deliberate." Sometimes the only way to get people to talk freely was to open a wound and look sympathetic.

"I've had a number of people tell me the same thing, but that doesn't matter now. Water under the bridge, as they say

—and now poor Theo—" He shook his head. "Hard to believe our annual fair has ended like this. We were supposed to all be sitting down to a barbecue this afternoon. Instead, we carried our kites back out for a tribute to Theo."

"I heard about the barbecue. I was standing at the local produce stand when a few of your club members were out looking for Theo. Were you part of the search effort?"

Aaron rubbed his forehead and winced. It seemed he was coming to the conclusion that his sunblock was patchy at best. "No, I didn't know they were looking for him. After my kite was damaged, I carried it back to the hotel room for repair. I can't be outside, especially on a sunny beach, for long. My skin burns easily. I've been in my room ever since, working on my kite. There was no sense in me coming out here to get sunburned when I didn't have one to fly."

"Yes, well, it seems your effort has paid off." We both stared up at the kite for a few minutes while it enjoyed a nice dip and turn. "Are you here on the island alone?"

"Yes, my wife wants nothing to do with my hobby. But then, she spends her day crocheting, and I want nothing to do with that hobby either."

"Men and women are so different, aren't they?" I glanced around. "I don't see Lyla. That was Theo's girlfriend, correct?"

Aaron looked around the beach. "You're right. I don't see her either. She's probably too distraught."

"How long were they together?" I asked.

"No idea. The club sends out emails and flyers and hosts the occasional online chat, but we live in different parts of the country. This annual event is the only time we see each other in person."

"That makes sense." I was surveying the sand for my next suspect. Sadie was standing under the shade of an umbrella. She looked upset. There was no sign of Owen.

"Is it true someone killed Theo?" Aaron asked. "We haven't gotten too many details, and I must say, the detective didn't seem to know what he was doing."

"You're very perceptive. And yes, Theo was murdered." I looked over at him. "Any ideas?" I asked.

Aaron shrugged. "Theo liked to cause trouble, so I'd say the police have their work cut out for them."

"Yes, I think they do, too."

twenty

AS I SURVEYED the sand and planned my next interview, Norwich arrived at the beach. Officer Harper was still at his side. Something told me it was Harper who suggested that all the club members stay on the island. It seemed far too logical and professional an idea to have come from Norwich.

I watched with amused interest as Norwich stood on the path, avoiding the actual sand, seemingly trying to decide where to start. Since he never wanted my input, I'd kept plenty of important nuggets to myself. I'd learned enough about the club and the interactions between some of the key players to know who could be considered a suspect. Was Norwich considering the entire club suspect? If so, then this might turn into a very lengthy investigation, and I doubted he could keep everyone here for that long.

Norwich again stared down at his shoes as if they'd been handmade with imported leather from Italy. I was sure that was not the case. Officer Harper shamed Norwich into leaving the path by stepping fully into the sand. Norwich followed reluctantly behind, taking time to lift each foot high and give it a little shake between every step. It was rather ridiculous considering there was nothing but sand as far as the eye could see.

The two policemen were heading toward the cluster of people who'd gathered to chat. I didn't recognize any of them as people on my suspect list, so I turned in the opposite direction and headed toward Sadie. I didn't see Owen with her, so it was my opportunity to talk to her alone. As I got closer, I saw that she was clutching a handkerchief. She was wearing dark sunglasses, so it was hard to tell if the handkerchief was a necessity or just for show. There seemed to be a lack of tears on the beach considering they'd just been told a club member was dead. And it seemed, of all the people in the club, Theo as president, would be the most well-known. Perhaps Aaron wasn't exaggerating when he said Theo liked to cause trouble. I'd seen some of that in the few days he'd been on the island.

"Hello, Sadie, right?" I asked. She looked surprised I knew her name but then she smiled.

"You were on the beach yesterday. You're friends with Johnny the parrot's owner." It seemed Johnny was going to be my ice breaker.

"That's right. You and your fiancé, Owen, are fans. I'm Anna, by the way." I turned on an appropriate frown. "What a shame about Theo Martin. He was club president, right?"

"That's right." She pushed her glasses up half an inch and dabbed her eyes with the handkerchief. I wasn't buying the act. She looked somewhat shaken but not as distressed as she'd like me to believe. "Theo spent so much time pulling together this annual fair, and now this—" Another quick blot under the eyes.

"Were you and Owen close to Theo?"

Sadie fidgeted with her sunglasses and looked briefly around. "Not really. Owen and Theo chatted occasionally. The topic was always kites. That was the only thing they had in common. And I'm not a kite enthusiast like Owen."

"When are you two going to be married?" This new topic made her less fidgety. A smile crossed her face. "One year from now. We've got a beautiful church selected, and the reception is at a nearby country club." She glanced not so casually at my ring finger and saw that it was bare. I'd kept my wedding band on for three years after Michael's disappearance, but eventually, I slid it off and put it in a box in my dresser. It made me sad to look at it every day. "I don't know if you've ever planned a wedding, but they take so much work," Sadie said with an exhausted sigh that was as dramatic and fake as the eye blotting. "I'm spending more time on the phone with vendors than I spend talking to friends and family. And it's so competitive out there. Everyone wants to hire the same florist and baker and band. The good ones are always booked way in advance."

I'd found her topic of interest, and she was certainly willing to tell me everything about her wedding plans, but I was far more interested in her side relationship with Theo. I just wasn't sure how to approach the subject without setting off alarm bells.

"My sister has had two big weddings, and yes, they take a lot of work." Of course, Cora had high-dollar wedding planners to help make calls and book reception staff. It was time to get her attention back on the reason we were standing out on the hot sand. I glanced around. "I expected to see more people out here."

"Well, Theo did occasionally rub people the wrong way. But I think most people are just avoiding more sunlight. They were out here all morning and then they were out looking for Theo—" Bingo, she'd landed on a much more interesting topic.

"Yes, I ran into some people looking for him. He was supposed to be setting up the barbecue."

"That's right. They might still have that later this evening since all of us are trapped now on the island." She produced a nice, irritated huff. "Owen and I were hoping to leave tonight, after the barbecue. We're lucky our hotel room was still available for the night."

Some of the people on the beach had started singing "Yesterday" by the Beatles. We stopped to listen for a moment.

"Theo loved the Beatles," she said it with a little roughness in her throat.

"Sounds like you knew him well after all," I noted. That comment made her fidget again. This time she spent a few seconds adjusting the straps on her sundress.

"Not that well," she said as she fussed with the dress.

"You don't happen to have a twin sister here with the club this weekend?" It was an odd question, and she gave me a confused look.

"A twin sister? I only have three brothers."

"I was just curious. Yesterday afternoon, right as the sun went down, I was riding my bike past the small bridge that spans between the island's two trails, and I spotted Theo on the bridge."

I paused to gauge her reaction, and it was profound. A dark pink blush rose up her neck and spread across her face. She reached for her dress straps again. Sadie was definitely a fidgeter.

"I'm sure he was out on a walk," she said with a shake of her shoulders.

"It's just that he was with a woman, and that woman looked remarkably like you."

The color in her face faded, and another shoulder shake followed. "You might have been imagining it. There are probably a lot of women who look like me at that time of day."

I shook my head. "I could have sworn it was you."

Her mouth pulled tight, and she looked quickly around. She spotted something behind me that made the color drain more. "You were mistaken," she said quietly through gritted teeth. A somber smile formed on her face. "Owen, darling, I wondered where you were. Remember this is the woman who knows Johnny the parrot." She spoke fast and nervously.

I'd gotten lucky. It seemed I'd be able to interview Owen as well. "I'm terribly sorry about your club president," I said to Owen. "Were you two part of the search party? I hadn't heard—who actually made the terrible discovery?"

Owen lifted his sunglasses. "I heard it was a local who found him, and as for the search party—Sadie and I spent the whole afternoon on a hike up at Calico Peak." He put his arm around her and pulled her closer. "Isn't that right, sweetie? She was tired on the way back, and I had to give her a piggy-back ride."

Sadie smiled along with the story. "My hiking shoes cost a fortune, but they were rubbing my heels."

Owen gave her a nice squeeze for that part of the story. If it was true, then the couple had an alibi for the murder. Opal would be disappointed that the crime of passion angle was out.

"How did you find the hike?" I asked.

"Not too bad," Owen said. "I've done a lot of mountain hikes, and your peak is small."

"That's true."

Owen squeezed Sadie again. She wasn't loving the attention. "Well, sweetie, we should join the others. They're going to sing a few more Beatles tunes." Owen turned to me. "Theo loved the Beatles."

"Yes, so I've heard. Well, I'll let you go then."

"By the way," Owen asked before I could step away. "Is that funny man with the big belly the island's detective?" There was no way to miss the amusement in his tone.

"Yes, that's Detective Norwich. He's here to investigate the murder."

Owen held back a grin. "Well, I hope he gets to the bottom of this. Most of us need to leave tomorrow, so we can get back to our jobs on Monday."

"I'm sure he'll crack the case soon," I said, and this time it was my turn to hold back a grin.

twenty-one

NORWICH HADN'T NOTICED me yet. He was busy talking to people here and there. It seemed he had no real plan, but that was usual for him. One thing was certain—the bright sun, heat and sand were getting to the man. His face was red, and he kept wiping the beads of sweat off his forehead. He was also still dealing with the aggravating issue of walking in deep sand in a pair of loafers. Something told me he'd be ending his series of interviews long before he got anything of worth from the club members.

My own investigation had hit a snag because two of my main suspects were not on the beach. I needed to talk to Lyla. I decided to try my luck at the hotel. Maybe she was in the restaurant eating a late lunch or drowning her sorrows with a glass of wine. The assumption was that she was too upset to come to the memorial on the beach, but I wondered if that was true. It seemed certain that Lyla knew about Sadie and Theo's affair. I'd witnessed their argument. Lyla was angry. But was she mad enough to commit murder?

I hurried back toward the harbor and across to the Frostfall Hotel. Its red roof and white plaster walls glistened in the afternoon sun. I reached the lobby and realized that, like everyone else, I was relieved to be off the hot sand. It was between regular mealtimes, so the restaurant was almost empty. I peered inside for a moment and then turned swiftly around, nearly smacking into a man crossing the lobby in a hurry. It took me a second to recognize him without his yellow hat and shark kite. He'd doused himself in strong cologne. Wesley Campbell was the other suspect I'd been looking for on the beach. Wesley and Theo had nearly come to blows over a kite fiasco, and Wesley made it obvious he didn't care for Theo. Still, was a kite accident motive for murder? I planned to find out.

"Mr. Campbell, how is your shark kite?" I'd found the kites were the easy jump off point for casual conversation. All of the club members were quite attached to their kites, like parents eager to talk about their kids.

I expected him to relay all his tales of woe and how he'd been busy repairing it. Instead, he acted somewhat cagey. He glanced around as if people might see him, and it seemed he preferred not to be noticed.

"The kite, yes, it's in my room."

"I figured it was still broken because I didn't see it at the memorial out on the beach."

"Uh right, the memorial. I was in my room. I had some business calls to make."

"On Saturday?" I wasn't fond of playing the devil's advocate, but when someone was acting as dodgy as the man in front of me, my little horns popped out.

Wesley's big chin jutted out defiantly. "I'm a hard worker. I rarely take time off."

His chin jut pointed out something else that I hadn't noticed before. There was a smear of pink lipstick on it. I reached up to my own chin. "You've got something on your chin, something pink."

He reached up and wiped at his face, transferring the pink lipstick from his chin to his thumb. His face turned red. "Don't know how that got there. Must have been something on the hotel towel. I certainly won't be giving this hotel a glowing review."

"Interesting. I've only ever heard good things about this hotel. It's sad to hear about Theo. I know everyone was looking for him earlier. Were you part of that?"

He took out his sunglasses and pushed them on his head. He was giving me a subtle hint that he was on his way out. "I'd taken a walk on the marina to look at the boats. I've been thinking about buying a sailboat. Then I had an ice cream. I had no idea that Theo was missing. Now, if you'll excuse me, I'm heading to the beach for the memorial."

"Then I won't keep you. By the way, have you seen Theo's girlfriend, Lyla? She wasn't at the memorial."

He reacted as if I'd slapped him rather than just asked him a simple question. He pulled back with an indignant scowl. "Why would I know that?" he asked brusquely. "I'm sure she's too distraught to join the others." He sidled past me. "Now, if you don't mind—"

I stepped aside and watched as he nearly raced from the hotel. The man was guilty of something, but was it murder?

My phone rang. It was Nate. "Hey, how is the riding?" I asked.

"Won't deny it, I'm having a blast. Wish we had mountain trails like this on Frostfall."

It wasn't what I wanted to hear. Darn Frostfall for not having mountain bike trails.

"Maybe you could plow a trail on Calico Peak," I said with forced levity.

"Everything all right?" he asked.

Obviously, word hadn't gotten to the mainland about yet another murder on Frostfall. I was sure our murder had been overshadowed by the PTK murder. I wasn't about to ruin his time by mentioning it. "All good here, so I guess I'll see you tomorrow, right? I'm looking forward to hearing all about your adventures."

"And I'm looking forward to having you in my arms." Nate always knew the right thing to say to make my knees turn to jelly.

"I'm looking forward to being in them." As I spoke, two of the club members entered the hotel with their kites and some handpicked wildflowers. It occurred to me they might be taking them up to Lyla. "Got to go, I'm—" I almost let slip that I was investigating a murder. "Uh, I've got a cake in the oven."

"Yum, chocolate? Is that for my homecoming?" He

laughed. "Can't wait. I'll let you go because I don't want it to burn. Love ya."

"You, too." I hung up. It seemed now I was going to have to bake a chocolate cake. Lies were always troublemakers. I dashed after the people with the wildflowers and managed to step onto the same elevator. I wasn't sure they'd give a complete stranger Lyla's room number, especially given there had been a murder on the island, so I decided to switch to stealth mode and follow them.

I smiled politely. "Aren't those sweet peas beautiful? The whole island has patches of them, and they smell like candy."

The woman lifted the bundle of sweet peas to her nose. "You're right. They do smell like candy."

They stepped out onto the second floor. I stepped out, too, pretending as if I had a reason to be on floor two, or in the hotel at all, for that matter.

I walked slowly behind them. When they stopped at the second door on the right, I had no choice except to keep walking. I turned the first corner and waited. There was a light knock and then a few seconds later the elevator doors opened and shut. I peered around the corner. They'd left the flowers in front of the door. The door opened and Lyla looked out. She spotted the flowers and picked them up before shutting the door. I pulled at the hem of my t-shirt to straighten it. It was time to leave stealth mode and put my investigator's hat back on.

twenty-two

I HAD a plan formulated by the time I reached Lyla's door. It was one thing to approach a suspect out in public, like at a memorial service, and then coax information out of them with some strategic chatting. It was another thing altogether to show up at a suspect's hotel room when I had no reason for doing so. I was going to need to be direct, but I planned to add in a little scare tactic to get her to talk. Hopefully, it would work.

    I knocked lightly and waited. It seemed she hadn't opened the door for the people with flowers, and there was a good chance she wouldn't open it for me. Then my whole plan would be worthless. I knocked once more, and surprisingly, the door opened. In an instant I noticed two important details. She was wearing the same shade of pink lipstick that Wesley had on his chin, and her room smelled like his cologne. At first it would be easy to conclude that Wesley had stopped by to check on her and that she gave him a peck on the chin as a thank you, only Wesley had been almost defensive when I asked if he'd seen Lyla. Now that defensiveness was making sense.

"Can I help you?" she asked. "I've already spoken with the detective if that's what this is about."

"I'm not with the police—not technically. But since you've already had a visit from Detective Norwich, I think it only right to warn you that he tends to jump to conclusions and make very fast arrests. Almost always the wrong person. And since you were Theo's girlfriend, I fear he'll be back here soon to arrest you." I felt guilty throwing that at her, but it was mostly true. I knew Norwich would make a clumsy arrest. I just didn't know who his next victim would be.

Lyla looked close to tears, but she blinked quickly to stop them. "I don't understand." Her bottom lip trembled. "I'm going to be arrested?"

"Not if I find the killer first. Can we talk?" Her frightened reaction to what I said had put her lower on my suspect list. I tucked away the reminder that it could all be an act, but I'd find that out soon enough.

Lyla hesitated and held onto the door as if she might just slam it in my face. "My name is Anna, and I live here on the island. I'm the one who found Theo's body. I help solve murders on Frostfall, and I'm working to solve this one."

"I suppose you can come in." She stepped back to let me in and then shut the door.

The first thing I noticed was Wes's bright yellow hat on the nightstand near the bed. He'd lied to me about not seeing Lyla. What else had he lied about?

"So, you're the one who found him?" There was a tremble in her voice. She seemed genuinely distraught, or maybe she was a good actress.

"I was walking back home, and I spotted some ravens—"

She reached for the dresser for support. "Were they—you know—pecking at him?"

"No, they hadn't gotten to his body. I thought it might have been an injured animal, so I walked to the river. That's when I found him."

"Did it look as if he suffered a lot?" she asked.

I shook my head. Dying by strangulation was certainly not an easy death, but I didn't need to bring that up.

Lyla sat on the edge of the bed. "I'm sorry, but this has been very hard on me. Theo and I had been together three years. His family will be devastated."

"I'm sure and I'm sorry. This must be very difficult for you."

She looked up at me. Her eyes weren't swollen from crying, but her lips were puffy, as if she'd been doing a lot of kissing. "You said the detective would arrest me? That's ridiculous. I didn't kill Theo."

"Unfortunately, Detective Norwich isn't great at getting to the real facts in a case. He prefers to take the lazy way out and arrest someone who knew the victim well."

Lyla pressed her hand to her chest. "That's not right."

"No, it's not. That's why I'm here. I'm trying to solve the case before Norwich makes one of his usual bad calls. When was the last time you saw Theo?"

Lyla rubbed her temple as if her head pained her.

"Shall I get you some aspirin?" I asked.

She shook her head. "I've already taken something. After the kite fair ended, Theo and I came back to the room. He rested and then showered. He told me he was going to help set up for the barbecue, but he'd put on a lot of aftershave, and I heard him gurgling mouthwash. He doesn't usually do that in the middle of the day." Lyla was trying to tell me something without coming right out with it.

"I know Theo was secretly meeting with Owen's fiancée."

Her chin dropped for a second. "My goodness, you do know a lot about what goes on here on the island." There was an accusatory tone in her voice. I'd managed to break down the stranger wall between us, and I didn't want to build it back up.

"It's a small island, and I'm out walking and biking all the time. I spotted the two of them together on the bridge yesterday."

Lyla nodded. "Okay. I'm sorry. I'm just a little on edge. I mean there's a killer on the island, and it's probably someone Theo knew." Her brows went up. "What about Sadie? Or Owen? That's who the detective should arrest, and I'll tell him that if he comes back to talk to me."

"I'm trying to get to the bottom of all this, and I have talked to Sadie and Owen. They had an alibi, but that brings me to my next question. Where were you during that time after the fair and before it was time to set up the barbecue? You saw Theo leave and knew he was going to meet Sadie. Did you follow them?"

She shook her head dejectedly. "I didn't need to see more.

I already knew they were seeing each other. It started about a month ago. I found some texts. They both worked in the same office building."

"Did Owen know?" I asked.

"Gosh, if he didn't, then he's a bigger fool than I thought, but I can't tell you that for sure. And, as for my own alibi—I was here in the room. I suffer from migraines, and the sun was getting to me. You should probably know—I told Theo we were through. I already had plans to move in with my sister. I told him it was over."

"How did he react to that?"

She dropped her head and sniffled. "He said he was fine with that and that our breakup was long overdue." She sniffled again. I pulled a tissue from the box on the dresser and handed it to her.

"So, you were in this room all afternoon?" I asked.

She wiped her nose and sniffled once more. "Yes, I took a shower and a long nap. But I was alone, so I guess the detective won't consider that a reliable alibi."

"No, but the hotel security cameras can corroborate that. If you don't show up on any footage, it proves you never left your room."

Lyla looked relieved. "That's good news. But will the detective bother to check the footage?"

She brought up a good point. Norwich probably wouldn't bother. "You make sure he does. And remember, I'm just guessing and trying to stay ahead of his next move." I realized I might be helping Theo's killer with my advice, but something told me Lyla wasn't guilty. However, there was still the pink elephant or in this case—the yellow cap—in the room to discuss.

"Lyla, I need to ask, and I'm not trying to stir up trouble or upset you—" I looked pointedly at the yellow hat on the nightstand.

Lyla's cheeks darkened. "That's mine. I wear it to keep the sun off my face."

"I know the yellow hat belongs to Wesley Campbell. I ran into him in the lobby, and he was wearing heavy cologne, the same cologne I smell in this room."

Lyla shook her head. "Right, I don't know why I lied about it. I guess you have me paranoid about being arrested for Theo's murder. Wesley dropped by to check on me. He must have left the hat." It was a clumsy save to say the least, and I wasn't done with the bomb drops.

"Wesley was also wearing the same shade of lipstick as you. Only it was on his chin."

Her cheeks darkened more, and she sighed loudly. "All right. We might have kissed a few times. We've always flirted with each other at these events, but Theo and I had always been in a relationship. I figured since we were broken up now, Wesley and I could act on the feelings we'd been ignoring."

"I saw Wesley and Theo nearly get into a fistfight on the beach. Was that spurred on more by what was happening between you and Wesley than the kite problem?"

She smiled weakly. "Two men in a fistfight over me? I wish. No, that was because of the kites. I don't think Theo knew anything about Wesley and me. He was too interested in himself to notice anything like that."

"Then I'll ask you one more thing. Do you think Wesley could have killed Theo?"

Her mouth dropped open. "Wesley? Well, no, no he wouldn't do that." She didn't sound terribly sure. "I don't know him all that well, but I don't think he's a killer." Again, there was little confidence in her tone.

I nodded. "Thanks for the chat, and I promise to solve this soon."

"I sure hope the detective doesn't come back to see me. I can't wait to get off of this island."

I nodded. "It seems a lot of people would like to leave. Thanks again." I walked out. Our chat had been successful in some ways, but it didn't answer my main question. Who killed Theo?

twenty-three

EVENING WAS FALLING FAST. I gazed out the kitchen window as I waited for the cake batter to come together. Fran had texted when Norwich left the island. He left with only his assistant, so there'd been no arrest. I assumed he was no further on the case than when he stepped onto the island earlier in the day.

"I smell chocolate," Cora said and sighed. "It is not easy to live in this house and keep my thighs thin."

"No one is forcing you to eat the stuff," I said. "And this cake is for Nate."

Cora huffed as she filled a glass with water. "I'm so glad the kite weekend is over. I'm going to sit in a bubble bath, then I'm going to pull on my best silk pajamas, and I'm going to stay in bed all day tomorrow."

"I wish I could spend a day in bed. I didn't have to serve them tea, but the kite club has worn me out, too." I poured the cake batter into the prepared pans. After my white lie, telling Nate I was baking a cake, I decided it was a nice way to brainstorm ideas on the murder. Baking, cleaning and painting nature always helped me clear my head.

After my talk with Lyla, I'd come away thinking she was not the killer. It did seem odd, though, that she'd been kissing another man merely hours after hearing that the man she'd been with for three years had been murdered. People do strange things when they're in shock, but it seemed especially weird. Of course, she'd broken it off with Theo earlier in the weekend, and he'd cheated on her with Sadie. Still, it seemed a brief period of mourning would have been proper. One thing was sure, I wasn't taking Wesley off the suspect list.

I walked over to the corkboard and pulled down Wesley's index card. I picked up the pen on the ledge of the board and started writing a note about his suspicious behavior in the hotel lobby. He didn't want to be seen. But by whom? Or was he feeling guilty about his smooch session with Lyla? The lipstick on his chin certainly embarrassed him. The pen I was using dried up halfway through the note. I scribbled it hard against the back of the card but with no luck.

I walked over to the small desk where I paid bills and made shopping lists. Cora had taken her glass of water out to the back stoop. She sat outside scrolling through her phone. I reached into the drawer for a new pen and my fingers grazed over the photo I'd stuck inside months ago. I'd been avoiding it successfully, but my quest for a new pen had spoiled that. I pulled the photo free. Months earlier, the man who'd purchased Michael's fishing boat, the *Wild Rose*, had tracked me down to give me something he was sure I'd been missing. He'd found it in the wheelhouse of the boat.

I looked at the photo. The twin boys were like matching cherubs in a Renaissance painting, with their round cheeks and smiles. There was no way to see who was holding them, but I knew who it was because of the message on the back. It was a short, simple and highly unsettling message. I turned it over. When I first received the photo, I'd read the sentence over and over until I couldn't stand to look at it. "Mikey, we need to talk," it said in red ink. The script was curly and feminine. I'd seen the handwriting and the nickname, Mikey, in Michael's high school yearbook. It hardly took my investigative skills to discover that Michael's high school sweetheart, Denise Fengarten, had sent him the photo. It helped that the same woman had mysteriously shown up in a few of my old wedding photos. She was not on the guest list. From there it was easy to assume she was the woman holding the twins. The next connection had been too heartbreaking for me to make, so I'd shoved the photo in the drawer and worked hard to wipe all of it from my head. Losing Michael had been traumatic and heartbreaking and all the horrid things that come with profound loss. Having Denise show up in wedding photos was bad enough. The picture of the twins had knocked the wind from me. There were so many unanswered questions, and at the same time, I wasn't sure I wanted any of them answered.

Cora came inside, and the cool evening breeze shook me out of my dark thoughts. I grabbed a pen and shoved the photo back in the drawer.

"I thought you'd stay out for the whole sunset," I said as I finished writing my notes on Wesley Campbell.

"I was but then I got that creepy feeling again." Cora said.

I spun away from the corkboard to face her. "What do you mean?" I was sure all that unexplained stuff was behind us. "Did you see someone?"

"No, not exactly, but it felt like someone was out there, in the shadows." Cora's dramatic moment was over. She waved her long fingernails. "Anyhow, I'm off to take that bubble bath. By the way, have you advertised for the new tenant?"

"Not yet and please stop dreaming that it'll be a rich, handsome, eligible bachelor. It won't be."

"I know," she said dejectedly. "Why would anyone want to live here on murder island?" She walked out of the kitchen.

I walked to the kitchen window and looked out. The sun had set, and the shadows of night were being filled in across the yard. There was no sign that anything was amiss. I hoped it was just my sister's imagination. My phone rang before I could wash my mixing bowl. It was Nate on FaceTime. It was nice seeing his handsome face.

"Hey, I wasn't expecting this," I said. "What's up?"

"Why didn't you tell me there's been a murder on the island?"

"Oh, that. I didn't want to mess up your weekend. One of the members of the kite club was strangled, and the killer threw his body in the river hoping he'd wash out to sea. A tree root grabbed him."

"I guess that means you had to spend part of the day with Norwich. I'm sorry I wasn't there."

"It's all right. I think he's even meaner when you're with me. If that's possible. He accused me of tying string around the victim's neck to make it look like a murder. He was really hoping it was an accident. In fact, he didn't want to get his loafers muddy, so he was about to call it that without even looking properly at the body."

"Not sure that guy could get any worse at his job." The room behind Nate moved as he walked across it and sat down on a chair. "So, you were the one to find the body? Of course you were," he added.

"I think I need to stop taking so many walks and bike rides around the island. I discover way more than I want to." Seeing Nate made my chest heavy with a feeling akin to being homesick. I loved my house, but it wasn't the same without him.

"Any suspects?" he asked.

I laughed. "You could say that. The dead man was engaged in plenty of drama in his short time on the island. Aside from a secret affair, there was a kite sabotage incident and a kite accident that resulted in a few fists being thrown."

"See, if you stopped walking around the island so much, you'd never get to witness all those important details."

"True. But would that be so bad?" I asked.

"Uh oh, someone is feeling blue. Anything else happening that you've neglected to tell me?" The earlier darkness, caused by the photo, hadn't gone entirely away.

I smiled at Nate. "I just miss you."

"I miss you, too. It's nice to get away for a while, but there's no place like home, especially with you in it."

"You get a gold star for that one." The timer on the oven went off. "Oh, I've got to get your cake out." I realized my misstep instantly.

He lifted a brow. "I thought you made the cake earlier? Or am I getting two cakes?"

I could continue the web of lies and tell him I was also making a carrot cake for his return but then I'd have to bake a carrot cake, and I was all baked out at this point. "I lied. I was investigating the murder, but I didn't want to tell you."

"So, I'm not getting a cake?"

I laughed. "Really? That's what you got out of my big confession? Yes, there's a cake. I'm a terrible liar, so I made you a cake."

Nate's smile was helping to banish all the dark thoughts for good. "Could you be any cuter, Anna St. James?"

"Hurry home," I said.

"I'll see you in the morning."

twenty-four

I WAS up before the sun. Huck and I headed out on a long, brisk walk. I wasn't in the mood to paint. I needed exercise, and I managed exactly that. Huck had to work to keep up with my pace. At least twice he jutted ahead, only to stop on the trail and give me a questioning head tilt about our speed.

We'd passed Olive's cottage and were close to Calico Peak when I heard a buzz overhead. It was Dirk's drone. As I drifted off to sleep last night, a question popped through my head. Had Dirk found anything else of interest in his footage? It seemed he'd had a broad view of the entire island all weekend with his flying robot. He'd picked up the secret tryst between Theo and Sadie, and his drone had had a brief, alarming encounter with the mystery man. Maybe he'd caught something else, something that would help move the case forward. At the moment, it felt stalled. I assumed the kite club members would be allowed to leave this afternoon, so time was limited. For the first time ever, I felt as if I might not get to the bottom of this one. I blamed it on all the other unexplained quirks of the weekend.

I found Dirk standing at North Pond Trail, the trail that led up to the peak. His drone was circling around North Pond.

"Morning," I called before I reached him. Huck trotted close to me as he stared up at the drone. A low growl rolled up from his chest. "It's all right, Huck. Just a manmade bird."

Dirk lowered his remote. "Hello. We meet again." He laughed. "I guess that's to be expected on a small island."

"That's very true." I stopped and we both watched as the drone buzzed over the pond. A few of the visiting ducks weren't too pleased with the intrusion on their morning float, but most of them ignored it.

"I guess it's been quite the weekend on Frostfall," Dirk said. "I saw the coroner leave with the body of the kite club president. Have they made an arrest yet?"

"Not that I know of, but our local detective is known for making impulsive decisions in that department. I was wondering—you didn't happen to find anything interesting on your footage from yesterday afternoon, say between noon and three?" I didn't have an exact time of death, but I knew Theo was on the swim beach all morning and that people were looking for him after lunch.

"Well, I showed you the man in the trees. Do you think he might be the killer? He sure seemed to be hiding."

"Yes, but that footage was shot on Friday, and Theo was killed on Saturday. There was a boat anchored in the harbor that I think might have belonged to the man in the dark cap. It was gone by Saturday morning."

"Right, then I guess it wasn't him. Speaking of caps, I do have some footage that I think fits that time frame." Dirk brought the drone in from its adventure around the pond. "There are so many beautiful sights to film on this island. I'm sorry to be leaving it."

"Come back in winter. It's exceptionally beautiful, mystical really, under a layer of fresh snow."

Dirk nodded emphatically as he pulled out a phone. "I'll write myself a reminder for that. And I'll bet there aren't any murders at that time of year."

If he only knew. I smiled. "Right. Now you said you had some footage."

Dirk scrolled through his phone. "Here it is. It stood out because the cap was bright yellow, and the landscape around it was so lush and green."

"A yellow cap?" I asked enthusiastically.

Again, the footage wasn't super clear because of the tree limbs and tall shrubs, but the man was near the river, close to where I determined the murder happened. More importantly, he was wearing a bright yellow cap. "Could you replay it for me?" I watched again as a big man in a bright yellow cap moved around in the landscape. There was no doubt about it. The man in the video was Wesley Campbell, and the time stamp was at half-past noon on Saturday.

"Didn't that man with the shark kite wear a bright yellow cap?" Dirk asked. "He's the guy who started a fight with Theo

Martin." Dirk's face smoothed. "Do you think it was him? Did he kill Theo because of the kite crash?"

"I don't know about that. Let me put my number in your phone." I took his phone and entered my number. "If you wouldn't mind sending it to me."

"So, it might be him?" Dirk asked as he sent over the video.

"It doesn't seem like much motive, but the two men didn't seem to like each other much."

Huck barked at someone. Aaron Wright, the owner of the dragon kite, stepped around the last bend on his way down the trail. He was wearing hiking boots and carrying a water bottle. "Hello, I didn't expect to see so many people out here at this hour. Beautiful sunrise, isn't it?"

We all took a second to admire the blush pink dawn stretching over the horizon. Aaron seemed quite happy considering the tragic ending to the kite fair. Right then, I was glad I didn't have a massive, infinite wardrobe like my sister. I'd pulled on the same jean shorts this morning. I reached into the pocket and felt around for the metallic strip of paper. I'd forgotten it when I spoke to Aaron at the memorial. Dirk's new video evidence had pushed Wesley Campbell to the top of my suspect list, but I'd found a piece of Aaron's kite tail right by the murder site.

"Dirk, right," Aaron said. "We met at the swim beach on Friday. I'm determined to buy a drone, so thanks for the tips on the best ones for the money." Aaron smiled with some recognition at me. "We spoke at the memorial," he said.

"Yes, I remember you because of your phenomenal dragon kite. I'm so glad he's up and flying again."

"Yes, thank you. However, I guess my kite being broken seems trivial now given what's happened," he said grimly.

"I suppose so." I reached again into my pocket as if I'd just remembered the silver tail piece was there. "By the way, I found this down by the river." I held the silver strip out, and he took it.

"Down by the river?" he asked again.

"Yes, it was quite far from the swim beach." He didn't seem too worried about his silver tail piece being near the river where Theo had been found.

He shoved into his pocket. "I'm glad you picked it up before a duck or bird tried to eat it. Along with flying kites, I'm very much a conservationist. The tail piece must have been carried away by the wind. I didn't notice because I was so upset about my kite being broken. Thanks for picking it up. A lot of people would have walked right past it."

There was no indication he was lying, and he certainly didn't get defensive like Wesley had done in the hotel. "Well, I'd better get back and shower before they kick me out of my hotel room. I've heard we'll be able to leave by two this afternoon. It's been a very trying weekend, and I think everyone will be just as glad to leave this annual event behind us. Have either of you heard whether or not there's been an arrest?"

"Not yet," I said. "Nice talking to you."

"You, too." Aaron walked away.

"Really nice guy," Dirk said. "Did you say you found that silver tail piece by the river?"

I'd found that Dirk was very smart and intuitive. I nodded.

"Gosh, that seems like a long way for that piece of silver to fly. But then, it *is* made for flight."

"That's true, and we do get some really determined gusts on this island." There'd been nothing in my chat with Aaron that raised alarm bells, even when he was confronted with possible evidence. "It was nice talking to you, and let me know if you find anything else on that footage."

He laughed. "It's funny, the actual detective never talked to me once. It seems like he should be handing his badge over to you."

I laughed, too. "Yes, it does seem like it." I waved and Huck and I started the long walk back home. I had a French toast casserole in the refrigerator. All I had to do was pop it in the oven to bake. With any luck, Nate would be home in time for Sunday breakfast.

twenty-five

OUR WALK home was slightly delayed by a pitstop at Olive's cottage for a dog treat. Huck had gone ahead, and I found him already sitting on her front stoop, tail wagging and waiting for Olive to hand it to him.

"Morning," I called.

"Oh, Anna, there you are. I didn't see you at first. I thought Huck had come here all on his own."

I reached the stoop and pressed my hands gently over the dog's ears. "Shh, don't give him any ideas. How are things?" Olive knew me well enough to know what I was asking.

"Fine. Never saw that man again."

"That's good. I think he just made a quick stop at the island. I'm sure he was perfectly harmless, but I'm glad he's gone." As I said it my phone beeped. I hoped it was Nate telling me he was on his way across the harbor. "I'll bring you some French toast casserole later. I'm going home now to put it in the oven. The sweet, buttery aroma usually wakes all the Sunday morning sleepyheads."

"That sounds delicious. I'll see you later. You, too, Huck. You've already had two treats."

Huck and I started off again. I pulled out my phone. It was a text from Frannie. I read it casually and then stopped cold to read it again. "Joe just called me from the *Salty Bottom*. That boat is back." It was the last thing I wanted to hear.

I wrote back. "Thanks for letting me know."

"Do you think it has to do with the murder?" she replied.

"Not sure." The timelines didn't add up. The boat was not in the harbor during the time of the murder. In fact, it had been long gone by then. The harbor was the only place a boat could dock or drop anchor. It was the only section of coastline that wasn't dotted with treacherous rocks and currents.

I decided to push the annoyance out of my mind. I wanted to solve the murder before Norwich allowed everyone to leave the island. Nate would be home soon, too, and while I liked to think I was a courageous, independent woman, it was nice to know he'd be back on the island.

All those thoughts helped me feel better about the day ahead. I wasn't going to let some indecisive boat owner get in the way of my investigation.

Huck trotted ahead and reached the boarding house before me. His loud bark startled me out of my thoughts. At first, it sounded like an excited bark, and I picked up my pace, sure the dog had seen Nate. But a few more barks were followed by a low growl.

My heartrate sped up along with my steps. I reached the yard. Huck was staring into the shrubs near the house. The hair was standing up on his back, and he continued to growl. The dog spotted me and raced to the back stoop to be let inside.

"You are so brave," I said wryly. I was resolved to get to the bottom of this. I'd had enough of the hide and seek game.

I let Huck inside and then turned sharply on my heels and surveyed the landscape. I didn't see anything, not even the tiniest movement of a branch. "You're on private property, so please show yourself," I said sharply. There was no reply. I marched down the steps with fists curled, hoping the intruder was watching so they could see I meant business. I walked to the spot where Huck had been standing. I considered that Huck might have scared them into hiding. He wasn't a great watchdog, but he could look plenty menacing with his hackles raised and his teeth showing.

"The dog won't hurt you. If you're lost, I can help. I won't leave until you come out. I'll call the police if I have to." That was an empty threat, but most strangers to the island had no idea that we had no local law enforcement. I stood patiently for a long time and then grunted in frustration. "Fine, you give me no choice. You're trespassing, so I'll call the police."

I marched back toward the steps, stopped once on the stoop to give them another chance and then went inside. I locked the back door behind me. I turned on the oven and pulled the breakfast casserole out of the fridge. Huck had slinked to his bed, but his head shot up suddenly as if he heard something outside.

I grabbed a kitchen knife and opened the door. The figure dashed back into the shrubs. I stood in the center of the yard with my jagged bread knife. "Please show yourself now!"

Adrenaline shot through me, and I took a step back when the thick foliage adjacent to the house moved. He stepped clear of the shrubs. The daylight illuminated his face beneath the black cap.

The ground beneath my feet seemed to give way, and my legs wobbled. The knife slipped from my fingers and landed in the dirt. Dizziness swept through me, and I couldn't remember how to breathe. Everything around me blurred as if I'd been caught in the center of a tornado.

"Anna." I'd almost convinced myself I was imagining the whole thing, but the voice was too real and too familiar.

"Michael?" The name cracked out of my dry throat.

"Anna?" My name came from the opposite end of the yard, another voice that was all too real and familiar.

I felt so unsteady, just turning to look toward Nate caused me to sway on my feet. I saw movement from the corner of my eye. It was Michael. He took a few steps toward me.

I held up my hand, but my arm, my whole body had started to tremble. "Don't come closer," I said. My voice was the only one that didn't sound the least bit familiar. It sounded distant, lost, breathless.

I looked at the man in the hat, the man I'd cried buckets of tears for, convinced that he'd been lost at sea for good. He was older, more leathery, but I knew his face as well as I knew my own.

I looked toward the other man, the one I'd only recently

given my heart to. Nate looked worried. His throat moved with a heavy swallow. "Anna."

"Give me a chance to explain," Michael said from the opposite side.

I had no idea how I managed it, but I got my feet moving, and once they took off, I ran right toward him, right to the arms I needed. My legs gave out as I fell into his arms.

"I've got you, Anna," Nate said before darkness swallowed me.

twenty-six

I OPENED MY EYES, but the room was so bright I shut them again. Had I forgotten to close the drapes, and why did my bed feel so uncomfortable? I opened my eyes again and gasped at the circle of faces staring down at me. Nate was amongst them. Huck was glued to his side as if he'd been sewn onto his best buddy with thread. It took me a second to clear the haze from my head.

"Why am I on the couch? Did I fall asleep down here?" My voice was gravelly, and my throat was extremely dry.

Cora was standing next to Opal. Her face looked unusually pale. "She doesn't remember," she said, as if I wasn't in the room.

Nate took hold of my hand. The look of concern on his face made me try to sit up in alarm.

Tobias's hand shot out to keep me from sitting up. "Wait until you get your bearings, Anna. You've had quite a shock."

"I'll say," Cora said again to Opal as if I wasn't there. "I thought I was looking at a ghost." She waved her hand in front of her face dramatically. "I've got to sit down." She pushed past Opal and plunked down hard on the couch in front of me.

I'd tried to shake the haze from my head, but as Tobias pointed out, I still didn't have my bearings. And why had he mentioned shock?

"What's going on? Did I fall?" I rubbed my temple. And then something hit me, the dream. "The last thing I remember is that—and this will sound crazy and a little pathetic—I dreamt that Michael had returned." I laughed lightly. "Just like that—back from the dead."

No one else was laughing, and their expressions grew grimmer. Cora wriggled nervously on the seat cushion. The movement pushed a wave of nausea through me. Opal and Tobias seemed to have a hard time making direct eye contact, so I turned to the one person I knew wouldn't fidget or avoid eye contact. As I looked at Nate, more of the dream was coming back to me, only it wasn't a dream.

Nate gazed down at me and gave a slight nod. "He's in the kitchen, but I can ask him to leave if you'd rather—"

"No, I need to see him." I attempted to sit up again. Tobias didn't stop me, and Nate helped me. The room spun for a second. Nate held me steady, so I didn't fall over face-first.

Cora stood up to give me some room. She crossed her arms. "This is just like Benny Ingram in high school," she said with a confident shake of her head.

I peered up at her slowly. Moving too fast made the room

spin more. "This is not at all like Benny Ingram. He stood you up for a date." (It was a traumatic experience for my sister that had obviously stuck with her.) "Benny didn't disappear from your life for nearly a decade only to show up alive and well on your—actually his—doorstep." That thought made me sit up straighter. "Maybe he's here to take back his inheritance."

"First, you should find out why he's alive and well," Opal said. "After all, everyone was certain the man had landed himself in Davy Jones's Locker. And now he's sitting at our dining table drinking a glass of water."

"You're right. He's got a lot of explaining to do."

"Understatement of the year." Nate helped me to my feet.

I walked bravely and resolutely toward the kitchen, but my feet froze in place before I stepped inside. Nate's hand took mine. "Do you want me to sit in there with you?"

I smiled at him and pressed my hand to his face. "No, we need to talk alone." I finally unfroze my feet and stepped into my kitchen, a place that always gave me great comfort. Not this morning. The oven had heated up the room and the breakfast casserole was still sitting, uncooked, on the kitchen counter.

Michael had taken off his black cap. His hair was thinner, and there was a touch of gray on the sideburns. He opened his mouth to talk, but I put up a hand to stop him.

"It's been nearly ten years. My turn first," I said. I realized there was no way I could stay standing. I pulled out a chair across from him and gave myself an indiscreet pinch to make sure this wasn't a dream.

"Years, that's how long I waited. That's how long I waited for this moment, where I sat at this table and you were sitting across from me, back from whatever harrowing experience you'd endured. But it wasn't harrowing at all, was it? I, on the other hand, grieved so much, I was sure I'd turn myself inside out with it." I picked up the pepper shaker, the nearest solid object to my hand, and threw it at him. He allowed it to smack him on the shoulder, then he placed it on the table.

"I'm sorry, Anna."

I laughed. It had that edge of hysteria I was feeling. None of this could be happening and yet, it was. Michael, my long-lost husband, was sitting across from me, wearing a wholly inadequate look of contrition on his face.

"If you're here for this house, I will get a lawyer, and I will fight you—"

Michael shook his head before I could finish. "The house is yours. You always liked it much more than me anyhow. It's the least I can do—"

Another dry laugh burst out. I made a mental promise that it would be my last. It was making me look unhinged, and I wanted him to know that I was still the strong, level-headed woman he married.

"Anna, please let me explain."

"Is it about the twins?" I asked. He reacted to my question as if I'd slapped him across the face. "So it *is* about the twins," I said.

"How did you know?" he asked.

I got up. I was glad the ground was feeling solid beneath

my feet again. I wasn't sure that the shock had worn off, but I was feeling stable. I walked to the drawer and pulled out the photo. I tossed it angrily in his direction.

He picked it up. "Where did you get this?"

"Apparently, when you abandoned the *Wild Rose* to convince me you were dead, you left this picture in the wheelhouse."

He placed the photo on the table and looked across at me. His gaze was familiar, but it didn't feel like a warm caress anymore. He was a stranger now. I could hear noises and low voices in the living room. If I knew my sister (and I did), she was leaning against the wall, eavesdropping with a glass pressed to her ear.

"Do you remember when I told you that I had a girlfriend in high school?"

I was way ahead of him, and I was feeling pretty cocky about it. I took the slump out of my shoulders. "Yes, clingy Denise Fengarten, who, oddly enough, showed up at our wedding. At the time I'd been so blissfully happy about marrying the man of my dreams I hadn't even noticed that a strange woman had snuck into the reception."

He'd come here to explain things to me, but he was looking more confounded by the second. I was glad to knock him off balance. He'd certainly knocked me off-kilter.

"My mom made some photo albums, and I saw Denise in a few photos. It took me a second to match her face to the girl in your yearbook. The writing on the back of the photo and her calling you Mikey clued me into the woman holding the babies. I must admit, a few unsettling theories went through my head, but I refused to let them take hold because I refused to let myself believe that you never loved me."

"Of course, I loved you, Anna. Sitting across from you right now has given me a terrible ache in my chest. I never stopped loving you, and I've missed you terribly, but..."

"But you staged your own death just to get free of me." I realized that part of me wanted to break down in sobs, but I refused to show him just how much he'd broken me. It had taken years, but I was nearly healed, and I wasn't going to let my progress slip away. Especially now, knowing he'd been alive all this time.

Michael scrubbed his fingers through his hair and shook his head. "You need to let me explain."

I took a deep breath. "I'm listening."

twenty-seven

IT WAS impossible to believe that I was sitting in my homey kitchen, my favorite room in the house and a place I'd sat for many hours, crying into a cup of coffee, lifting my face at every noise, hoping that it was Michael returning from sea. Now he was sitting here, at our dining table, still looking as broad-shouldered and formidable as ever. However, everything about him was different. This wasn't the man I fell in love with. He was someone unfamiliar.

Michael's face dropped. He seemed to be searching for the right words. It seemed the whole, sordid confession was going to be harder than he thought. I was glad to see him squirm.

After a long moment, he lifted his gaze. "About a month before the wedding, I ran into Denise at the mainland harbor. I'm certain now that the run-in wasn't accidental. She insisted we have a cup of coffee and talk about old times. I saw no problem with that. I told her I was getting married and that some of my old friends from high school were throwing me a bachelor party at the Steak and Stein. She knew some of them, so that's why I mentioned it. She showed up to the bachelor party. I was pretty drunk by that time, and you know how those things are—"

I shook my head. "Never been to a bachelor party, so no, I don't." I stared at him harshly because I knew where this was going next.

"We got together that night," he said quickly, as if that might soften the blow. It didn't. "I swear it was the only time it happened, and I was drunk."

"You mentioned that already. Not an excuse," I added.

"You're right. I thought that was it, and I hoped to someday gain enough courage to confess the whole thing to you. Then Denise showed up at the reception. I realized then that she was dealing with a lot of mental health issues. There were subtle signs in high school, but she'd really taken a sharp turn for the worse. I asked her to leave the reception, which she did, and again, I thought that was the end of it. Then nine months later, after you and I had started our life together, I was docked in the mainland harbor. Someone left that photo taped to the window of the wheelhouse. I took a paternity test to make sure the boys were mine." For a second, the grief and shame on his face vanished and he smiled. "Trevor and Parker are my whole world."

"Why didn't you just tell me what happened? Why didn't you tell me you were leaving me for Denise and your sons? I would have been heartbroken, but I would have gotten over it. Having you vanish was so much harder, so much worse. I guess the cowardly way out was easier."

"No, it wasn't that," he insisted. "I begged Denise to get some help. She had those two little boys, but she grew more unstable every time I talked to her. She told me if I didn't come back to her that she'd give them up for adoption or worse."

I gasped. "My gosh, what a monster."

"I had no choice except to take the boys and disappear. They wouldn't have been safe here, and I worried that Denise might do something to—" he paused.

"To me?" I asked.

"Yes, she talked about you all the time."

A moment of silence followed, and I was thankful for it. I needed to absorb everything he was saying. "Where is she now?"

"She lives about thirty miles inland from the harbor. I spoke to her mom. She's the only person who knew my plan. She said Denise has gotten some medication and seems to be better. She doesn't even ask about the boys."

"Where have you been all this time?" I asked.

"Newfoundland," he said with a shrug. "Good fishing up there. It's a little rugged, but it's a nice, quiet place to bring up the boys. There's a woman up there, we have a mutual thing. We take care of each other, but it's mostly a friendship."

"You don't have to sugarcoat it for me. I've moved on," I said.

Michael's gaze drifted toward the living room. "Yes, I see that," he said wryly.

It was my turn to shrug. "I won't sugarcoat either. Nate is a tenant here, and over time we've fallen in love. I don't know where it will go from here because a certain person has made me very wary of committing my heart to someone. Which reminds me...Excuse me, everyone will be hungry for breakfast." I wanted him to know that he'd broken me once, but he wasn't going to break me again.

I pushed the casserole into the oven and popped my head into the living room. The entire crowd, Huck included, dashed away from the doorway. Opal and Tobias dropped clumsily onto the couch with guilt splashed across their faces. Nate and Huck pretended to be interested in the view outside the window. Only Cora remained at the doorway. She put her hands on her hips. "Some story."

I rolled my eyes. "Breakfast will be a little late due to unforeseen circumstances." As I said it, I realized it might not have been all that *unforeseen*. I hurried back to the kitchen.

Michael was putting away his phone. He looked embarrassed. "Just making sure the boys are all right. They can be a handful, especially when I'm not around."

"You've been here before," I said. "On the island, since your disappearance." I sat down again.

"I was here on Friday morning, anchored out in the harbor. I took a dinghy to shore. I kept my hat and glasses on, not sure if some of the boaters would recognize me. I saw you."

"You *watched* me," I said sharply.

He nodded. "Yes, but only because I was trying to work up my nerve to talk to you. I chickened out."

"Seems to be a theme with you." I couldn't stop the anger yet. I figured eventually I'd see his side of the story and try to understand it, but for now, I was feeling beyond hurt.

"I deserved that." He'd finished his glass of water. Normally, I was a better hostess, offering visitors coffee or iced tea, but I wasn't feeling all that hospitable. I reached for his glass.

"I'll get you more water. I'd ask you to stay for breakfast but—well—I don't want you to stay."

"That's all right." He chuckled. "I thought your sister, Cora, might crown me with that frying pan on the stove. She's still as fiery as ever."

He was trying to lighten the mood, but I wasn't ready for any humor or nostalgic talk. "When I asked if you'd been to the island before, I wasn't talking about Friday. I mean in the past few years. There have been times—moments when I was sure someone was watching me, watching the boarding house. I once even thought I smelled your cigar."

Michael nodded weakly. "I came here once about a year ago. It's a long boat ride down from Newfoundland, but I thought it was time to tell you everything. I watched you. You looked content and happy. I decided not to throw your life into turmoil again, so I left without ever showing myself."

"It was only the one time?" My head was in a cloud still, but as I flipped back through my memory bank, it seemed I'd felt someone watching me or the house several times in the last eighteen months.

"Yes, like I said, it's a long ride, and my boat isn't great. I bought it way back when—" He paused. "It was my escape boat. I pushed the *Wild Rose* ashore and climbed aboard the second boat."

"There was a huge, expensive and very official search. I imagine you'd be on the hook for that bill if the Coast Guard knew the whole thing was staged."

"I'm sure you're right. But you can't squeeze blood from a turnip. I left everything behind. I went to Denise and told her I was taking the boys to the park. Then I put them on the boat, and we traveled north to the cottage I'd rented in Newfoundland. We get by with my fishing, and I keep them fed and sheltered and happy. That's the only thing that matters to me now."

I should have taken some solace that at least Michael was a good dad and he did what was right for the boys, but somehow, I'd had to take the brunt of all his mistakes.

"The birthday card," I said suddenly. "On my fortieth birthday, I received a birthday card with no return address and a quickly scribbled birthday wish. There was a piece of dried purple larkspur inside the card."

Michael looked at me in confusion.

"I had purple larkspur in my bridal bouquet. It wasn't from you?"

"No, I'm sorry. I didn't send it." His mouth pulled tight with worry. "You have no idea who it came from? Maybe it was from someone here on the island, and the flower choice was a coincidence." It seemed he was trying to come up with an explanation more for himself than for me.

"No one ever stepped up to ask if I'd received it. You're thinking it's from her. From Denise?" I asked. "Just how much danger am I in?"

Michael shook his head. "None. I'm sure of it. Her mother assured me she's doing better with medication, and I'm not entirely convinced it came from Denise. But that's why I disappeared. That way you and I no longer had any connection."

The kitchen was beginning to fill with a delicious aroma, and I realized that my stomach was empty and I was hungry. The shock had been great, but as I absorbed Michael's confession, I had a smidgen of sympathy for the man. His whole life had been upended, and he'd sacrificed everything for his sons. But all of it stemmed from his mistake of letting Denise back into his life. He'd made one majorly bad decision, and from there, his life fell like a pile of dominoes. Mine had fallen, too, for a long time, but now I was building those dominoes back up, and he had no part in my life anymore.

"After they declared you dead, I got the deed to the house. I love this house, and I've made it into a successful business. More importantly, the people who live here, my sister included, filled the huge, painful void you left behind. They're my family now, and we all love this place."

"I promise you, Anna, I'm only here to finally tell you what happened. The house is yours. You'll probably never see me again." It surprised me that his promise made me sad. I'd waited so long for his return, and now he was back, but it was only for a short time and then he'd be gone again, vanished and seemingly swallowed up by the vast ocean.

"This whole thing has me torn between hating you and being relieved that you are still alive, but I think it's for the best that we part and never see each other again. I do wish you the best, and I hope the twins grow up to be healthy, happy adults." I was relieved he took my cue that our conversation had ended. There were so many more things I could ask him and probably plenty he could ask me, but I'd heard the parts I needed to hear, and that was the end of it.

Michael stood up. "Huck doesn't know me anymore," he said sadly.

"You've been gone a long time, Michael. We're standing in the same kitchen we stood in so many times, and I barely know you. It's been long enough that we're almost strangers. Time does that. Just like it heals some of the greatest wounds. Have a safe trip back to Newfoundland."

Michael stared at me for a long moment. "Thank you, Anna. And I wish this had all turned out differently."

"Me, too."

twenty-eight

MY WONDERFUL *FAMILY* was so supportive. Opal and Cora got breakfast on the table. Tobias brewed a pot of coffee, and Nate swept the front porch, a chore I usually saved for Sunday afternoon.

The room was quiet and a little tense as we all sat down to breakfast. Everyone seemed to be tiptoeing around me, something I needed to put an end to fast.

"Everyone, I want to say thank you for your support. All of you mean so much to me. But I'm fine. I've absorbed most of the shock. And I'm sorry if I alarmed all of you by fainting. I've honestly never fainted before, but seeing Michael sent me into a tailspin. When he stepped out of the shrubs, it was one those weird, surreal moments like when you're woken out of a deep sleep, and it takes a minute to decide whether you're awake or still in a dream. But now I'm fine. A huge, heartbreaking mystery that has plagued me for nearly ten years has been answered. Michael is not dead, and he's living in Newfoundland with his two sons." Nate had sat down next to me. I reached over and took his hand. "While I've gone through something terrible, I think it's all worked out in the end. I've got all of you, and I can't imagine being happier than I am right now."

Tobias lifted his glass of orange juice. "Here's to our wonderful Anna, and may she always be happy."

"Here, here," everyone said as they lifted their glasses.

"Here, here," Nate said quietly. He added a nice wink.

We ate in silence for a moment, everyone absorbing the incredible events of the morning.

"Do we have to worry about that crazy woman, Denise?" Cora asked. She was rarely subtle with her inquiries. I also knew now that she'd eavesdropped on the entire conversation, and I could call her on it, but she wouldn't care.

Her question got everyone's attention, even Nate's.

"Michael said she's on medication now, and according to her mom, she's doing better. One of his reasons for leaving me and the island was to cleave any ties between us, so Denise wouldn't bother me."

"Chivalrous," Nate muttered wryly.

I decided to ignore it. There was no reason Nate needed to like Michael or feel conciliatory toward him, and I would never ask it of him. And he was right. Michael's affair with Denise could have caused me a great deal of trouble. The woman threatened to get rid of her own children. She was certainly an unstable individual.

"So, that woman, the one who crashed your wedding reception, sent that birthday card?" My sister was also relentless when she had something in her craw.

"No idea," I said. "We'll probably never know, and that's all right. Michael lives in another country, and we've agreed that our lives have parted permanently. All I care about is that I get to keep the house. *We* get to keep the house. And soon we'll have a new tenant." It was time to change the subject.

It felt as if this day had already been five years long, and it wasn't even noon yet. I was still trying to decide if I'd let anyone else know about Michael's visit. I supposed I would have to. There was no way Cora could keep this secret and then Sera would be upset that I didn't tell her. Sera had been my shoulder to cry on and most supportive friend after Michael's disappearance. She needed to know. So did Frannie, Molly and Olive. But I needed time to process all of it first.

"Cora, I'm going to ask you a giant sister-to-sister favor," I said.

"You know you can borrow anything in my closet…that fits," she added. I loved my sister, but she could be annoyingly catty and at the entirely wrong time.

"I'm sure this will shock you, but I'm not interested in borrowing your clothes."

Opal snickered behind her coffee cup. I was glad that the conversation and atmosphere in the kitchen was no longer guarded. The best thing for me was for everything to get back to normal. Eventually, Michael's visit would become "Remember that day when Michael returned?" Time had a way of making everything big and alarming seem much smaller and more manageable.

Cora hadn't noticed the slight. "What's the favor?"

"Please don't tell anyone about Michael being alive. It'll be a great shock to everyone, and I want to deliver the news myself once I've given it some thought."

Cora bit her lip, a sure sign that she wasn't entirely sure she could keep that promise. "But I work all day with Sera—"

"Cora, please," I said.

She nodded. "Right, my lips are sealed…but it won't be easy." She took a sip of juice and looked over at me. "How come only I have to promise? What about everyone else at this table?"

I sighed, but I knew I didn't need to explain myself.

"Fine," Cora muttered. "I won't say a word."

A loud knock at the door startled everyone and sent Huck, who was still on edge, under the table.

Nate shot up. "I'll get it." Another frantic knock and we all startled again.

"My gosh, it couldn't be him, could it?" Cora asked. "Maybe he's decided he wants the house after all."

I waved my hand to hush her and followed Nate to the front door. He opened it. Aaron Wright, the man with the dragon kite, was standing on the porch. His face was pinched and pale, and he looked extremely upset.

"Can I help you?" Nate asked, but I rushed past him. After the shock of the morning, I'd forgotten all about the murder.

"Aaron, what's happened? Has someone else died?" I asked and led him inside.

Nate stepped back reluctantly.

"It's all right, Nate. Aaron is a member of the kite club. What's going on?" I asked a visibly distraught Aaron.

Aaron raked his fingers nervously through his hair. "I've been told to come to you. People in the hotel, locals, said, 'You have to go see Anna St. James.'"

"Was someone else murdered?" I asked again.

"No, thank goodness." Aaron finally took the deep breath he needed. "This morning, I got word that I was the number one suspect in the murder of Theo Martin, and I've been warned not to leave the island. The detective is coming to arrest me. I didn't kill Theo. I promise it wasn't me. Everyone said that you could find the real killer and get me out of this." He gave me a pleading look. "Can you help me?"

I nodded. "Yes, I'm already working on it. In the meantime, cooperate with the detective, answer all his questions, call a lawyer if you'd like. This wouldn't be the first time he arrested the wrong person."

"Probably won't be the last," Nate muttered.

My words did little to ease Aaron's worries. "I've seen these kinds of things on television. People get arrested and convicted and sent to prison for life for a crime they didn't commit. Please. I need your help."

"I'm going to get right on it." I walked him to the door. "I know it's hard, but try not to stress too much. With any luck, I'll have this wrapped up before Norwich even makes it back to the island."

Aaron took my hand and shook it. "I can't thank you enough. You'll let me know how you get on?"

"Yes, I will."

Aaron left the porch, and I shut the door. Nate looked at me with a raised brow. "So, are you close to finding a killer?"

I laughed dryly. "I wish."

twenty-nine

I WASN'T happy there'd been another murder on the island, but at the same time, I was relieved to have something else to focus on. The morning had drained me of energy, but I felt better once I stepped out in the fresh air. With the mystery man and boat explained, and in a way I could never have imagined, I felt much more relaxed hiking around the island, even if there was a killer somewhere on Frostfall.

Dirk's drone footage of Wesley near the river had given me a good starting point. I had to take Aaron's word for it that he wasn't the killer. The fact that Norwich had zeroed in on Aaron Wright helped convince me that was the case. I could almost always cross a suspect off the list if the person became Norwich's target. He always managed to pick the entirely wrong person to arrest, and I doubted his track record on being a spectacular failure had changed.

I noticed a few kites down on the beach. It seemed the kite club was still on the island…at least for now. I headed that direction hoping someone on the beach would know where I could find Wesley. A man and woman, standing close to the path, were flying some beautiful butterfly kites.

"Excuse me," I called. "Can you tell me where I might find Wesley Campbell?"

The woman pointed across the beach. Sure enough, Wesley was strolling along the shore wearing his bright yellow cap. I held out hope that the bright yellow cap was my ticket to solving the case. I wanted to talk to him alone, but Lyla was walking with him. They weren't holding hands or walking arm in arm. That would have been too obvious. I assumed most people had no idea that Wesley had swooped right in after Theo's death to court Lyla. Getting rid of the original boyfriend was certainly motive for murder.

Lyla told me that she had always flirted with Wesley at these events, but she'd been with Theo. If Wesley had strong feelings for Lyla, then maybe this time he decided to make his move and do something to rid himself of the Theo problem. The only flaw with that theory was that Lyla had already broken up with Theo. Wesley and Lyla would have already been free to start a relationship. The murder wasn't necessary. Unless, of course, Theo confronted Wesley about it and told him he would stand in their way no matter what. But I'd seen Theo with Lyla at the tea shop. She was visibly distraught about their relationship, but he didn't seem to care.

I reached the couple, and they looked less than happy to see me. Was it because I knew they weren't just two friends strolling on the beach, comforting each other?

"Miss St. James, right? That's your name, isn't it?" Wesley asked. He sounded a touch accusatory. "I hear you're the person they go to on this island to solve murder cases. Never heard of anything like that, but I guess that's why you were harassing me in the lobby of the hotel."

"And me." Lyla's tone was far less friendly today.

"You probably don't need to waste any more time on this, because from what we've heard, the detective is returning to the island today to arrest Aaron Wright," Wesley said dismissively. I didn't let his tone deter me.

"Yes, but I'm not convinced that Aaron is the killer." I walked along next to them, whether they liked it or not.

Wesley's chuckle was cold. "I guess you consider yourself more adept at this kind of investigation than an actual homicide detective."

I circled in front of them to stop their progress and looked straight at Wesley. "In this case, yes. Norwich rarely gets it right. That's why the locals count on me to solve these things, and frankly, I'm pretty darn good at it."

Lyla couldn't hide her smile. She looked up at Wesley. "Women are capable of doing 'men's work,' Wes."

Her comment ruffled him enough that his chest puffed out. "I know that. I'm not from the Middle Ages." Was there already tension in the new relationship? It was one thing to flirt with someone, someone whom you thought you could never have. It was another thing for that flirting to morph into something more serious.

"Wesley and I had nothing to do with Theo's murder," Lyla said with nothing at all to back up her statement.

"I'll cut to the main reason I'm here." I looked at Wesley. I was glad we were standing on a beach with other people around. I could question him without worry. I'd found myself in dangerous situations when I'd confronted a suspect with what I considered to be irrefutable evidence, and I had some of that. I pulled out my phone and explained as I scrolled for the footage. "I'm sure you've seen or even met the man with the drone. He's been taking a lot of footage of the kites and all the scenery on the island. He shot this footage in the same time frame as Theo's murder."

They both leaned in to look at the video. "That's your yellow hat," Lyla said blithely.

Wesley didn't seem terribly upset about being caught on tape either. He straightened and shrugged. I expected a more profound reaction, but maybe he was good at keeping a poker face.

"So, I took a walk to the river. That's hardly a crime."

"I know this island really well, and you happened to be standing very close to the place where Theo was murdered."

Wesley was finally comprehending what I was suggesting. "You think I killed him? Why would I do that?"

I looked at Lyla and then back at him. "Well, we could start with the obvious."

"It couldn't be Wes." Lyla's giggle bordered on nervous, and she stepped slightly away from Wesley. It seemed she'd started a relationship with a man she didn't really know, and that was showing now. "Tell her, Wes," she said with little confidence.

"Lyla, of course I didn't kill him. You can't possibly think that." Wesley seemed hurt that she'd so quickly stepped away from his side. His nostrils flared as he turned back to me. "You're starting trouble and looking in the wrong place. I had no motive to kill Theo. Lyla had already broken up with him."

Lyla nodded. "It's true. Theo didn't care when I told him I was going to start seeing Wes. He was already moving on, too, with Sadie."

"What about the fight on the beach?" I said. "Your kites tangled, and the two of you fought until the others stopped you."

My phone rang. It was Fran. She usually texted, but I was in the middle of something and had to let it go to voicemail.

"That? That was just two angry men. I was mad that our kites collided, but I was mostly angry at Theo because of the way he treated Lyla. She was very hurt, and I couldn't stand to see her like that."

Lyla's expression softened, and she moved back to his side and took hold of his arm. "So, you were fighting about me? That's so sweet." It seemed Wesley had redeemed himself, at least in Lyla's eyes, but I still wasn't sure about him.

"Look, I'm sorry if I came off as rude," Wesley said. "I walked down to the river, sat there and watched a pair of mallards for a few minutes and then returned to the walking path. There was no sign of Theo and no sign of anyone, for that matter."

I nodded. "I'm just trying to make sure the detective arrests the right person. Thank you for talking to me."

I pulled out my phone and listened to Frannie's message.

I sensed the urgency in her voice before she even said two words. "Anna, you need to call me as soon as you get this message."

I stepped off the sand and dialed Fran's number. She answered on one ring. "Anna," she said frantically.

I stiffened. "What's happened?"

Frannie paused. Also unlike her. "I don't know how to say this, and it's probably all just Joe's imagination, only he seemed sure of it. Joe saw something, *someone* in the harbor today." She paused again. "I shouldn't tell you this over the phone."

I knew then what had her in such an agitated state. "It wasn't Joe's imagination," I said calmly. "Are you sitting down?"

I heard her plunk onto a chair. "I am now."

"The mysterious boat in the harbor belongs to Michael, my long-lost husband. It turns out he's not dead or lost, just relocated." There was no response. "Fran?"

"Just wait until I get my hands on that man," Frannie said.

"There's a long explanation for his disappearance, but like you said—it's a conversation better left for an in-person chat. In fact, I'll have you and Sera and Molly for coffee later, so I can tell all of you at once. It's not a story I want to tell often. In the meantime, if you could keep the shocking part, about Michael being alive, to yourself, I'd greatly appreciate it."

"When can we meet? I'll be on pins and needles until then."

"Soon but first, I have to solve a murder."

thirty

THE WILD AND unbelievable news was out. Even though I asked both Frannie and Cora to keep it to themselves, it was the kind of news that would be impossible to keep secret. I almost preferred the notion that the news would be out before I sat down with my three closest friends to explain everything. I wasn't great at delivering big, sensational news.

I'd left Wesley and Lyla behind on the beach and ran into yet another couple, one that was even more in the center of the drama. Owen and Sadie were sitting on the boardwalk bench eating ice creams. It seemed everyone was out of the hotel now, most likely waiting for permission to leave. The ferry was going to be busy this afternoon. I was sure Norwich would come and arrest Aaron and then strut around like a proud rooster letting everyone know that the culprit had been caught and that they were free to leave the island.

Sadie smiled at me as I walked toward them. They looked like a perfectly happy couple, as if they didn't have a care in the world. I still had no clue if Owen knew anything about Sadie's affair with Theo. If he didn't, then he certainly had little motive to kill the man.

"We've gotten word that the detective is on his way to arrest Aaron," Sadie said with a touch too much glee. I hadn't focused on either of them much because they had an alibi. They were both hiking up the peak at the time of the murder. Were they covering for each other? It was hard to know for sure.

"Yes, I've heard."

Owen shook his head slowly. "I can't believe it, but then Aaron was extremely upset about his kite, and we all witnessed the debacle. It was deliberate." These two were certainly happy to put this whole event behind them.

Sadie pulled out her phone. "I'm anxious to get back and try on this new engagement ring." She held up a photo of a large, pear-shaped diamond ring. She twisted the one on her ring finger. It was considerably smaller and less impressive. "I've never been happy with this one, so my wonderful fiancé ordered me a new one. It's more than a karat with a platinum setting."

"It's lovely." Was that my answer to whether or not Owen knew about the affair? Was he just trying to win back her love with a big diamond?

"Thanks. That's why I'm anxious to get back home. I need to get it fitted."

"Well, congratulations and safe trip home." At the moment, I had nothing else to ask them. They had an alibi, and they seemed perfectly happy with each other. I was at a wall. The people I'd suspected were all claiming innocence, either with plausible alibis or forthright insistence that they didn't do it. Aaron had done the same, but was he using me? Had he heard about my ability to clear names and decided that he'd use me to do the same for him, even if he was the killer? I had a lot to ponder, including what I was going to tell my friends when we sat down to coffee. I hadn't heard from Sera, so maybe Fran had kept things quiet for now. And since Cora had decided to spend her day off luxuriating in bed, I was sure she hadn't spoken to Sera.

I meandered up Calico Trail, past the swim beach and toward the peak, mostly to get my blood flowing and hopefully, some brilliant next steps. A buzzing sound pulled my attention to a tall red maple just off the trail. Dirk's drone was stuck in the tree. Its buzzy motor was still running, but it wasn't going anywhere. It surprised me because I'd seen Dirk move his drone deftly through much tighter landscape. I headed toward the drone and then heard a low moan coming from somewhere in the thick foliage.

I hurried into the greenery and made my way around some shrubs toward the river. I could hear the water rushing over rocks. It was loud, but I could still hear the moaning. I headed toward it and gasped when I spotted Dirk on the ground. His head was bleeding. The remote was broken on the ground next to him.

I rushed to his side and crouched down. He was moaning in pain and trying to open his eyes. I moved so that I blocked any harsh sunlight. The wound on the side of his head looked bad.

"Dirk, it's me, Anna. Try and stay awake. I'm calling for help." I pulled out my phone. It was rare when we needed an emergency airlift from the island. There was a helicopter pad east of Finnegan's Pond on the southern tip of the island. I called for emergency services and returned to Dirk. He was in bad shape, but at least he was alive.

"Anna," he said weakly. "What happened? My head is killing me."

I glanced around and spotted a large sharp rock with blood on it. "Someone hit your head with a rock. Try not to move but keep talking to me. You'll be fine. The helicopter is on its way."

"I didn't see it coming," he said weakly. "Where's Robbie?"

"Robbie?" I asked.

"My drone."

"I'm afraid he got himself stuck in a tree, but we'll get him down for you. Did you see or hear anything? Do you know who did this? Try and think back to the attack."

He groaned again, and his eyes drifted shut.

I touched his hand. "Dirk, try and stay awake. I know it's hard."

"My phone." He reached blindly toward the pocket on his jeans. He patted the pocket. "They took my phone. I was facing the river, and I heard footsteps in the brush. Before I could turn around, a sharp pain shot through my head and everything blurred. I dropped to the ground, and I felt them rummage through my pockets. But I didn't get a look at them."

"So, someone stole your phone? It has all the drone footage."

"Yes," he groaned again. "Maybe it was Wes, with the yellow hat, or the guy with the black hat. I only wanted to get footage of the island. That's all." His eyes drifted shut.

I lightly tapped his face. "Stay awake, Dirk. It's important."

"I'm trying," he said weakly.

I sat with him for a good twenty minutes, keeping him awake. I called Nate to meet the helicopter at the pad and told him where to find me at the river. Dirk was thankfully still conscious when I heard the helicopter fly over the island.

"Help is here," I told Dirk. "They'll get you to the hospital, and you'll be fine." I sure hoped that was the case. "And I'll take care of Robbie until you're ready to get him."

"Thanks, Anna, you're a nice lady. Was that a helicopter?"

"Yes, that's the quickest way off the island. You'll be at the hospital in less than thirty minutes."

A weak smile tilted his mouth. "I've never been in a helicopter before. I just wish I was feeling better, so I could enjoy it."

"You'll be feeling better soon."

I stood up so I could see the heads of Nate and the medics when they got to the trail. My phone rang. It was Nate. "We're just crossing the bridge to Calico Trail."

"Keep on the trail until you get to the big bend in the river. I'll keep an eye out for you and wave when I see you. Look for the big red maple with the drone buzzing in its branches." I hung up and returned to Dirk. "Help is almost here. And I apologize for all this, Dirk. Our island is not usually so dangerous."

"They're lucky to have you here, Anna."

Minutes later, the medics had pushed their way through the foliage to tend to their patient. He was still conscious as they rolled him away on the gurney. It wasn't until they were out of sight and Nate put his arm around my shoulders that I took the time to cry. What a day it had been.

thirty-one

FRANNIE TEXTED that Norwich had arrived on the island and that she was anxious for our coffee chat. I sent a group text to Sera and Molly asking them to come to the boarding house for coffee. I added that I had something to tell them. Both women sent responses asking what was going on, but I told them I needed to talk to them in person.

My gaze kept flitting to the corkboards. Dirk's attack had certainly added a new layer to the case. It wouldn't take anyone long to commit such a terrible crime, and since everyone had still been on the island this morning, my suspect list hadn't narrowed. I doubted that Dirk's assault was a separate incident. He obviously captured footage that someone didn't want recorded.

I brewed a fresh pot of coffee and cut slices of chocolate cake for my guests. It was a little silly to be setting up a nice coffee visit considering the bomb I was about to drop, but chocolate cake always made every moment in life easier. The weekend had me spinning. Aside from the shock of Michael's return, I was dealing with a murder that I couldn't seem to solve. And now a perfectly nice, innocent man had been injured.

The first knock at the door pulled me from my thoughts. Nate had gone on a bike ride to test his new shocks and to retrieve Dirk's drone and remote. Cora assured me she had no plans to leave her bed, and Opal was involved in a Boris Karloff movie marathon. Tobias was in the front room reading a book. He knew I'd called my three best friends over to break the news and gave me a nice, supportive hug before heading off with his novel.

I opened the front door. Sera and Molly had arrived together. Both were smiling but hesitant. Frannie, on the other hand, reached the yard behind them. She had her fists balled and a look of determination on her face.

"What's going on?" Molly asked. "I saw the helicopter arrive." She put her hand to her chest. "Was it someone we know?"

"No, that incident has nothing to do with my news. One of the visitors to the island, a young man with a drone, was attacked down by the river." I led them all to the kitchen.

"Yum, chocolate cake," Sera said. "Uh-oh, this must be big news if you baked a chocolate cake." Her eyes lit up. "Did Nate propose?" she asked excitedly.

Molly was about to jump on the celebration wagon, too. Only Fran kept her expression grim because she knew this wasn't an engagement announcement.

"No, this isn't about a proposal," I said quickly to douse that line of thinking.

The women sat, and I served them coffee and cake before sitting down across from them. Molly caught sight of my murder case corkboards. "I hear Norwich is making an arrest. Did he actually solve a case this time?"

"I don't know," I said. "I can't seem to get a handle on this one."

"Is that why we're meeting?" Sera asked and then seemed to want to take back her question. "No, why would you do that? You'll get this solved. I'm getting the sense this is something much bigger."

Frannie was getting anxious. "Maybe we should let Anna explain instead of jumping to all kinds of conclusions." She said it sharply enough to garner angry looks from both the other women.

"No, don't be mad at Fran. She already knows my news, and she's upset. I'll explain. There's been a strange boat in the harbor, and people were worried about it," I started. I'd rehearsed this speech in my head a few times, but now I was searching for the words.

"I thought the boat left," Molly said. "Was that the killer?"

Frannie had far less patience than most people, and she'd reached the end of her small strand of patience. She set her coffee cup down loudly. "This has nothing to do with the murder. Let Anna explain."

Molly and Sera now looked worried. "What is it, Anna?" Sera asked.

I didn't want to draw this out longer than necessary, so I

jumped right to the point. "The equally mysterious captain of the boat turned out to be Michael."

"Michael who?" Molly asked.

Sera seemed to understand. Some of the color drained from her face. "Michael?" she asked shakily.

I nodded. "Yes, Michael, my long-lost husband."

A stunned silence followed, at least for as long as Frannie would allow. "So where is he? I need to give him a piece of my mind, and it's a very large piece at that."

Sera seemed to be taking in the news all while trying not to fall over in a faint.

"Sera, are you all right?" I asked. "I know it's a big shock. I fainted for the first time in my life this morning, and I still haven't recuperated from it."

"But how?" Molly stuttered out. "Michael was declared dead. He vanished. His boat was found."

"She knows all that," Fran said harshly. "Is he trying to take back this house?"

"Fran, please, your anger isn't making this easier. I'm mad, too, but I do have somewhat of an explanation from Michael. And he's gone now. I don't think I'll ever see him again, and that will be for the best. As for the house, he insisted it was mine to keep. He's started a whole new life in Newfoundland with his two sons."

Sera was mostly silent. I'd cried on her shoulder so many times about losing Michael. She knew the depth of my despair better than anyone.

I turned and looked directly at her. "I've absorbed all of this and will keep processing it, but I'm fine. I have my life now, and I'm happy, and nothing from the past can change that." I faced all of them. "You guys helped me through the trauma of losing Michael, and I'll never forget that. Michael had a brief affair, and it resulted in twins. The mother was unstable, and he needed to take the boys far away. At the same time, he wanted to cleave ties with me for my own safety."

Sera took a steadying breath. Some of her color had returned. "It was her, wasn't it? The woman you said turned up in your wedding photos? Michael's high school girlfriend." I'd told Sera about the wedding photo and the twin photo.

"Yes. You could say those photos helped me absorb the impact of Michael's story a little easier because somewhere deep in my chest, I knew that Michael had been unfaithful and that he'd fathered the twins."

"What a jerk," Frannie said.

I nodded. "Yes, he made the mistake in the first place, so it's impossible to forgive him for that."

"I don't understand why he thought he had to go to such drastic measures," Sera said. "We do have a little something in this country called a court system. He could have gotten custody."

"True, but I got the sense that there was an urgency to getting the boys away from their mom. She threatened to give them up for adoption 'or worse.' Those were Michael's words."

"Worse?" Molly's color faded now. "What a lunatic."

"Are you in danger?" Sera asked.

"I need a photo of this woman, so I can make sure she doesn't get on the ferry," Fran said.

Admittedly, there had been times when I was out on the island or even in my own yard when it felt as if someone was watching me. Michael said he was here only one other time, and it was easy to believe that because Newfoundland was a good distance away. Fran's suggestion sounded reasonable.

"I'll ask my mom to send me the wedding photo with Denise in the background. Otherwise, all I have is her yearbook photo."

"So, you are in danger?" Sera reiterated.

"No, I don't think so."

"That doesn't sound reassuring," Molly said. "If the woman was willing to harm her own children, there's no telling what she's capable of."

"Yes, but I no longer have any connection to Michael. That's why he faked his death and traveled up the coast to Canada. She has no reason to bother me." I said it with confidence that I wasn't necessarily feeling. "Besides, I'm not worried. I've got my Moon River family and all my Frostfall family here for support, and I'm pretty sure if Denise Fengarten tries to step on the *Salty Bottom*, Captain Fran will summarily toss her overboard."

The laughter helped break some of the tension my news had delivered. We spent the rest of the time eating cake and talking about things other than Michael and murder, and I, for one, was glad of it.

thirty-two

MY FRIENDS LEFT with bellies full of cake and wary smiles. It seemed it was just as hard for them to believe what had happened as it was for me. I still looked back at the morning as surreal, like a movie, instead of my real life.

I was cleaning up the plates and cups when Nate walked in the back door. He was carrying the drone and the broken remote. It was purely my imagination, but the drone, Robbie, looked sad, like a lost puppy. Seeing the equipment reminded me that Dirk had probably left his belongings in the hotel room.

"Thanks for getting the drone out of the tree. Was it hard?"

"Nah. When I was a kid, I was a champion tree climber."

I smiled. Nate was the main reason I'd held myself together so well after Michael's surprise visit. Nate reminded me how much my life had changed for the better since his arrival. "Do they give out actual awards, you know, championship medals for tree climbing?"

"No, the championship thing was mostly in my head. I did, however, earn neighborhood hero status by rescuing Rachel Hanover's kitten from an old oak tree."

"I can just picture little Nathaniel Maddon standing with his big smile for the local paper photographers. Was Rachel holding her kitten and giving you a peck on the cheek as they snapped the picture?"

"No one called the local paper, and now that you mention it—I feel cheated."

"Have another slice of cake. That'll help," I said.

"Good idea." He sliced himself a thick chunk of cake, poured a glass of milk and sat at the table to eat. "Have you heard how the kid is doing? The one with the drone?"

"The medics who flew to shore with him told me they wheeled him right into the trauma unit, but he stayed awake and alert the whole flight. Was even asking the pilot all kinds of questions, so I'm sure he'll be fine. Seeing his drone reminds me—Dirk probably left some belongings at the hotel. I'll go collect them and bring them here. That way he can pick up everything when he comes for the drone."

"If he ever wants to step foot on Frostfall again." Nate plowed a bite of cake into his mouth.

"Don't you follow Opal's lead. She thinks there are way too many murders on the island."

Nate raised his brows as he chewed the cake.

"You've got frosting on your chin, and yes, we have more than our share of murders. I do agree."

He wiped his chin and swallowed. "Thank goodness the island comes with its own highly skilled homicide investigator. And she makes the best chocolate cake." He plowed in another bite.

"This investigator is feeling less than skilled at the moment." I hung up my dishtowel. "I'm going to the hotel to collect Dirk's things. With any luck, I'll run into a suspect or two, and they'll have the words 'I'm guilty' written across their forehead in black ink. I'll even settle for red ink."

"Wouldn't it be nice if that was the way these cases worked. Do you need me to come with you?"

"No, you should rest. You returned from your adventure and stepped right into another adventure. I'm sure you could use some quiet time."

"Actually, that does sound good." Huck was sitting at his feet under the table. The dog released a loud doggie sigh to let us know it sounded good to him, too.

"This whole thing has exhausted Huck," I said. "I'm sure he'll stick by your heels for the rest of the day."

"Did Huck get along well with Michael?" Nate asked. "He seemed upset by his presence."

"Now that you ask that—not really. Huck tried to be his best buddy, but Michael just never made the effort." I thought about a few times when Huck would be waiting anxiously for Michael to return, and Michael would brush past him without so much as a pat on the head. When Michael and I married, I'd never once questioned my decision to say yes to his proposal. Now I was rethinking it a lot. It seemed I'd married the wrong man after all.

Nate got up, and as I predicted, Huck trotted next to him toward the stairs. It made me smile. Maybe this time I'd gotten it right.

I was tired myself, but not too tired to make another trip to the harbor and to the Frostfall Hotel. There were a few kites still on the beach. It seemed the kite club hadn't left the island yet. There was no sign of Norwich. Sometimes he used a conference room in the hotel to question a suspect before taking him back to the mainland. It sounded much more involved and thorough than Norwich's usual investigation, but I knew he used the hotel as his island precinct when he had people to interrogate. Had Norwich actually had second thoughts about Aaron being the killer? If so, then Aaron just moved up a few spots on my own list.

I reached the front desk. A young woman stood behind it, finishing up something on the computer. Many of the hotel employees were from the mainland. They took the ferry to work and back home. The woman had hair that was tinted pink on the tips, and her nametag said "Willow." She wasn't a local.

"Can I help you?"

"I sure hope so. Hello, Willow, I'm Anna. I live here on the island. I was the person who called the airlift for the man with the head injury."

She scrunched up her face. "I heard about that. Poor guy. He was staying here at the hotel."

"Yes, as a matter of fact he was, and when I found him, I promised him I'd take care of his personal belongings."

She nodded along affirmatively. "Great. They were waiting

to clean out room 35. The manager isn't here today, and none of us knew what to do because his stuff was left behind."

"Well then, I guess I'm here to help you," I said cheerily. This could have gone either way. Some staff were very by the book and would never have given me a key to the room, but she was handing it over before I could finish talking. I decided to push my luck a little farther as I gripped the key. "By the way, is it true that Detective Norwich is here at the hotel?"

Willow leaned closer to talk in a quiet voice. "He's interrogating a suspect in Conference Room A. I don't know exactly what's going on because I'm new here, but it seems to be about a *murder*."

"That's what I've heard, too. Thanks for the key. I'll bring it back after I collect his things." I headed across the lobby. I didn't notice any of my suspects milling about the place, but I hoped they were still on the island. If Norwich was interrogating Aaron here, then he might be trying to shore up a case against Aaron before he made an arrest.

I headed up to Dirk's room and opened the door. His things were already packed and ready to go. He was planning to check out before the attack. There were a few empty soda cans on the nightstand and some food wrappers in the trash; otherwise the room was cleaned up. When my gaze swept past the complimentary notepad on the dresser, I noticed someone had written a note. The note was no longer on the pad, but they'd pressed hard enough with the pen to leave an imprint on the next sheet of paper. I could only assume Dirk wrote the note. It was probably just a reminder or a phone number, but I decided to try and decipher it. I carried the notepad to the window for better light. Some of the letters were faint, but I could read parts of the note.

"I need the money to…or I will show him the vid…"

It was easy enough to fill in some of the blank letters. Was Dirk blackmailing people for drone footage? If so, then that put him in a whole different light. Maybe he wasn't an innocent bystander after all. Who was he blackmailing? The note didn't say, but I'd bet a big pile of money that he was assaulted by that same person. The question was—did that have to do with the murder, or was Dirk's assault a whole different crime? I hoped I could get my answers before everyone left the island.

thirty-three

FRANNIE'S HUSBAND, Joe, was running the ferry today. I spotted him sweeping the deck. A number of bags and suitcases were lined up in an orderly fashion on the dock. Joe spotted me and stepped off the boat. Joe was a big, imposing man with a generous and sweet smile. Years on the ocean had left his face crisscrossed with deep lines that only added to his kind smile. Today his expression was more sympathetic than usual. Joe had fished with Michael many times, so he knew Michael well and was torn up about his purported death.

"Anna, how are you holding up?"

"Actually, I'm good. I'm wondering if the weight of it is still trying to take hold and then maybe I'll fall apart, but right now, I'm trying to solve a murder." I looked at the line of bags. "I assume these belong to the kite enthusiasts?"

"Yes. I made them put them down in order, and that's the order I'm taking them back across. Once Norwich gives them permission to leave the island, that is. There's no telling when that'll be, with the way that man runs his investigations. He was here to make an arrest, and everyone checked out of their rooms thinking they were going to be heading back to the mainland. Then Norwich pulled the plug on that idea. I let them put their bags here. The kites were a different thing altogether. There's no way to park a kite on a windy dock."

"That's right, there are no kites here." I rubbed my temple. "Don't know how I missed that."

Joe cleared his throat and gave me a fatherly look. "Uh, I think we can excuse that after the morning you had."

I smiled. "Thanks, Joe. I guess everyone must be down on the beach with their kites waiting for word from Norwich. I'll head down there and see if I can talk to a few more people before the killer makes a clean getaway."

"I thought Norwich had the killer in his sights. He's at the hotel with the suspect right now, or at least that's what I've heard."

"He has a suspect in his sights, but I'm pretty sure the real killer is still wandering around the island."

"This island is lucky to have you, Anna. And I'm sorry about what happened. I always liked Michael, but I've got to say—now it seems I didn't know the man at all."

"None of us did, Joe. Well, I'm off to catch a killer."

"Be careful," Joe called.

I waved to him as I left the dock and headed in the direction of the swim beach. There were only a few kites in the air, but as I reached the path to the beach, I saw that most of the club members were there with grounded kites. Some were gathered in groups, no doubt talking about the murder and Aaron being a main suspect.

Lyla was sitting alone on the sand. Wesley had switched to an olive-green cap. He was standing with a few other men near the water. I'd shown him the incriminating footage from Dirk's phone, and Dirk was attacked shortly afterward, but there didn't seem to be enough time between when I spoke to Wesley and Lyla and when I found Dirk by the river for Wesley to have done it. And Wesley hadn't been bothered or anxious about the footage. He'd gone for a walk, and that was all there was to it. Lyla had started a relationship with Wesley just hours after learning her ex-boyfriend had been killed. She also seemed uneasy when I showed them the footage, as if she wasn't entirely sure she knew Wesley well enough to trust him. I certainly knew what that felt like. I'd married a man who I didn't know at all.

I walked over to Lyla. She felt my shadow drop over her and shaded her eyes to look up. "Oh, it's you." I'd heard that disappointed greeting more than I cared to.

"Do you mind if I sit?" I asked.

"I don't mind, but I don't have much to add to Theo's murder."

I looked over at her in question as I sat down.

"I know you're investigating the murder, but you aren't actually a cop."

"You heard right." I decided not to get into semantics with the woman. I needed to find out who killed Theo before everyone left the island.

"I guess you and Wesley are anxious to leave," I started.

She shrugged. "I don't know about Wes, but I'm ready to go. This has been a terrible weekend."

I stretched my legs out. There was no reason I couldn't get a little color on my legs while I was busy investigating a murder. The sand felt soft and warm under my bare legs, and I wished, suddenly, that I was just out on the beach enjoying the sun and trying to sort out everything that had happened in my personal life this morning instead of trying to solve a murder.

"But at least you were able to start that relationship with Wesley," I reminded her.

A short, dry laugh shot from her mouth. "Turned out flirting with him was fun, but he's not for me." She dusted some sand off her hands with a swipe of her palms. "We've already parted ways. Besides, we live about five hundred miles away from each other. Long distance relationships are hard, but they're impossible if neither person is really that into the other person."

"And that feeling is mutual?" I asked.

"Yes, we both realized the fun was more in the secretive flirting. We figured out it wasn't going to work. And after what happened to Theo, it all felt wrong. People were talking and giving us dirty looks. I just need to be alone for a while."

"You'll probably enjoy that alone time more than you realize. Since the two of you aren't together, can I ask you one thing?"

"No, I don't think Wesley killed Theo," she replied,

cutting off my question. "Besides, I've heard Aaron did it. We're all waiting for the arrest to be official, so we can leave."

"It's true Aaron is being questioned by Detective Norwich, but the man who took the drone footage was attacked. Someone took his phone."

"That's terrible, but I guess if you're spying on people, you're bound to upset someone."

Wesley glanced our direction. He didn't look pleased to see me sitting next to Lyla.

"Wesley didn't like Theo, and like he said, he didn't like the way Theo treated me, but he wouldn't have killed Theo. I wasn't the love of Wes's life, and he wasn't mine. I think there has to be a little more passion for someone to work up to murder. And I was mad at Theo and glad to be done with him, but I could never kill anyone. I freak out if I see a dead animal in the road. I can't imagine seeing a dead person."

It was a weak alibi, but I didn't get the sense that Lyla had killed Theo. And as she pointed out, Wesley's motive lacked passion. The fact that they'd gotten together and called it off in less than a day was proof of that.

"The man with the drone—will he be all right?" Lyla asked.

"I think so. And you're right, spying on people is a good way to get in trouble."

"Well, Wesley and I were together most of the day. We finally came to the conclusion that this wasn't going to be a thing when we set our things down on the dock. He couldn't have attacked the man."

"No, I didn't think so. The timing was off." I glanced

around and spotted Owen with some of the other men. "Have you seen Sadie?"

"Fortunately, no," Lyla said sharply. I'd momentarily forgotten that Sadie had been one of the reasons Lyla broke up with Theo.

"Well, have a safe trip back." I stood up and dusted off my legs.

"Do you happen to know when we'll be free to go?" she asked.

"There's no telling what's going on in the head of Detective Norwich," I said with a smile.

thirty-four

I SPOTTED Sadie sitting on a bench on my walk back from the beach. She was browsing through her phone. As far as I knew, Owen was still on the beach talking to some other club members.

"Hello, Sadie," I said.

She looked about as receptive to my presence as Lyla had been. At least she skipped the "Oh, it's you" greeting.

"Hello." I didn't bother to ask if I could sit next to her because it was a public bench, and I was running out of time and patience with this case. I seemed to be bouncing from suspect to suspect and getting absolutely nowhere. Maybe Norwich had his man after all. "I spotted Owen on the beach. I guess you're anxious about getting to that jewelry store for the ring fitting." The topic of her new engagement ring made her perk up. Having your fiancé buy you a second engagement ring because the first wasn't impressive enough sounded like something my sister would do, only I doubted Owen was rolling in money like Cora's fiancés. Or maybe I was wrong. Either way it made her look spoiled and made Owen a bit of a sucker, especially given that Sadie had cheated on him. Of course, I still had no idea if Owen knew about the dalliance. I hoped to find that out.

"It's interesting that Owen bought you a second ring. Some women have a hard time just getting the first one," I said with a laugh. "I guess he's just extra generous."

She wriggled uncomfortably on the bench. "He likes to keep me happy. Nothing wrong with that."

"There certainly isn't," I said.

"I suppose Owen has forgiven you, then, for the affair with Theo." As the day wore on, I grew bolder, and that one just shot out without much thought or planning.

Sadie sat up straight and tugged on the hem of her tight tank top. "That was nothing, and Owen knows it."

"So, Owen did know about you and Theo?" I prodded. The first time I talked to her about it, she acted as if Owen had no idea she'd kissed Theo. That had left me with no motive for Owen, but this might change the whole dynamic of the case.

"I didn't say that. I mean, he might have. I don't know. Either way, what happened between Theo and me was just a silly mistake, and Owen loves me. That's all that matters." A phone rang in her purse even though she was holding a phone in her hand.

I looked pointedly at her purse. "You bag is ringing."

She grew very flustered and hopped up from the bench. I followed. "That's Dirk's phone in your purse, isn't it? You hit

Dirk on the head with a rock, so you could get his phone and the incriminating drone footage."

She stopped and dropped her face into her hands. A sob followed.

"Dirk was blackmailing you, wasn't he?"

She lifted her face and whipped it my direction. "Yes, the little weasel." She sobbed again. "I didn't mean to hit him so hard, but I was angry. He told me I had to give him five hundred dollars or he'd show Owen the footage of Theo and me in the trees. Little snoop. He's going to get himself into big trouble with that drone. I only meant to knock him senseless, so I could grab his phone." She sobbed again.

"I can see why you were angry at Dirk, and obviously, he should never have blackmailed you, but you nearly killed him."

"I know and I'm sorry about that. He'll be all right though, won't he?"

"Uh, that I can't tell you. He was conscious when he reached the hospital, but head injuries are serious. If Owen already knew about your tryst with Theo, why not call Dirk's bluff and tell him to go ahead and show the video to Owen?"

It took her a second to collect herself. "Dirk threatened to send the footage to the whole club."

"Did you kill Theo?" I asked. For a second, I thought I'd finished the case. Now I wasn't so sure.

Sadie gasped as if I'd slapped her. "Never. The detective has already made an arrest. Aaron Wright killed Theo because Theo ruined his kite. Theo was like that, petty, childish, even vindictive."

"So maybe he deserved to die?" I suggested.

"Of course not. That's ridiculous."

"As ridiculous as Aaron killing Theo because he broke his kite. Aaron managed to salvage the kite, after all. I don't think he had motive to kill Theo."

Sadie looked fretful at something past my shoulder. I glanced back. Owen had left the beach and was heading toward us. His expression turned to a scowl when he saw it was me talking to his fiancée.

Sadie's demeanor changed, too. She went from visibly distraught to more confident with a straight posture and a forced grin. "Please don't tell Owen about our conversation," she said through gritted teeth so she could maintain the grin. She waved to Owen with that same fake smile. That was when I noticed that her hand was very small, like the rest of her. The rock she used to hit Owen would never have fit in her one hand. She didn't look strong enough to crown someone hard enough on the head to nearly kill them.

Owen was still a good distance off and carrying his kite slowed his pace, so I turned back to her. "It's a good thing I was walking across the bridge earlier, or I might not have found Dirk lying there at the base of the bridge."

"I suppose so." Her face twitched a few times, and she fidgeted with her purse. The phone had stopped ringing. Now I knew she was lying. She was protecting the real attacker.

"Why don't you hand me the phone? Otherwise, you'll be walking around with evidence that implicates you in the attack."

"I'll take care of it," she said quickly. She was worried I'd hand the phone to the police, and they'd find another set of fingerprints on the phone that didn't belong to Dirk or to Sadie. It seemed the ring had been a bribe rather than a gift to his loved one. But how could I make sure I had the killer? A brilliant idea popped into my head.

"What's going on?" Owen asked. He eyed me with suspicion. "So, it's true you run around pretending to be a detective or some great sleuth. Well, you're a little out of the loop. The real detective is about to leave the island with his suspect." He smiled at Sadie. "We just got word that we can leave the island, and I, for one, can't wait to be off this lump of sand."

"Oh, it's not all that bad," I said. "After all, we have lots of scenery and then there's Calico Peak, a tourist favorite. That's right. You two walked up to the peak already."

Owen scoffed. "It's hardly a hike or a peak." He glanced back toward Calico Peak. "More like an anthill."

"Well, we enjoy it. How did you like the Buccaneer Trail? It's named after our pirate history."

"It was all right," Owen said. "Now if you don't mind, Sadie and I want to get in line for the ferry."

"Then you saw our famous lover's rock? The big granite boulder halfway up the trail?"

"Yeah, you've seen one rock, you've seen them all," Owen muttered.

"But it has that big heart-shaped dent in it." I looked toward Sadie for confirmation about the unusual rock.

She smiled weakly. "Yes, it was a very pretty rock. Now, we should go, Owen."

I nodded. "Of course. Have a safe trip."

I watched them walk toward the ferry and glanced in the direction of the hotel where a small commotion seemed to be taking place. Norwich was leaving the hotel with Aaron Wright in handcuffs. I'd badly wanted to spare him the humiliation of being walked out in handcuffs. Now the image would be permanent in the minds of all his club mates. I'd promised to help him, but I'd fallen behind. I supposed I could excuse myself on this one. After all, it had been a trying day.

And aside from his short humiliation, Aaron would soon be free. I had the killer in my sights. He was heading back to the ferry, hurrying along his fiancée. He'd paid for Sadie's silence with a big diamond ring. Owen had just blown a huge hole in his alibi, but he had no idea…yet. The two had used a hike up Calico Peak as an alibi, only I knew they'd never gone up the trail. Buccaneer Trail did not exist and unless I'd missed it on one of my many hikes to the peak, there was no heart-shaped lover's rock. The only thing that disappointed me was that Dirk wasn't innocent in all of this. And he'd nearly paid with his life.

thirty-five

"STEP ASIDE. Official business. We need to be on the first boat out!" Norwich yelled as they reached the docks. Norwich's big belly strained against his shirt as he strutted toward the ferry. The officer with him, a new assistant, held Aaron's arm as they led him toward the ferry. Aaron's face was ruddy with splotches of white, and he looked close to tears. Owen and Sadie were standing with their bags. Owen's big red parrot kite fluttered in the breeze. Everyone held tightly to their kites making sure they didn't escape in a rogue gust of wind. It would have been a colorful, amusing sight if a murderer wasn't standing amongst them.

"Detective Norwich, you have the wrong man," I said. My gaze flitted in Owen's direction. He was scowling at me.

"Not you again, St. James," Norwich groaned. "Why don't you go home and leave the investigations to the professionals?" My statement had gotten everyone's attention. Everyone moved in closer to find out what was going on. Sadie and

Owen stayed back. Sadie's mouth was pulled tight, and she looked upset.

"Aaron Wright did not kill Theo Martin," I said loudly and clearly. I hadn't solved the case fast enough to keep Aaron from suffering this terrible humiliation, but hopefully, this would help. Some of the crowd had pulled out their phones to record the scene. Frankly, I could have done without it, but I needed to forge ahead before Norwich hauled away the wrong person. I'd been worried about a lack of evidence, but something came to me during my chat with Owen and Sadie. They were being blackmailed, but not because of a secret kiss.

"You don't know what you're talking about," Norwich said.

"Detective, how on earth can you let her talk to you like that?" Owen asked.

That question, of course, enraged Norwich more. He was being humiliated in front of spectators, spectators with phones. His nostrils flared, and he yanked the toothpick from his mouth, a sure sign that he was about to blow his stack at me. (I'd daydreamed more than once about that actually happening—his stack being blown.)

"St. James, go home now before I arrest you for obstructing justice!"

Only Owen clapped. Sadie seemed to shrink back from the whole scene. It was dawning on her that she'd made herself an accomplice to murder, and she was going to be doing some jail time. That ring would have to wait.

I pointed, rudely, in Owen's direction. (Occasionally it

was necessary to break etiquette rules.) "Owen Perez strangled Theo Martin because Theo was secretly seeing his fiancée, Sadie Moore. He found out they were seeing each other, then he followed Theo down to the river and strangled him with kite string." The crowd gasped and murmured amongst themselves. I heard more than one person say, "That makes so much more sense."

"This woman is crazy," Owen snarled.

"Unfortunately, he bought off Sadie's silence with a diamond ring," I said. "Isn't that right, Sadie?"

Owen glared at her. She was speechless and pale.

"You can probably get a lighter sentence if you tell the police everything you know," I said to her as if there weren't twenty people standing right there with us. Wesley and Lyla had joined the group, too. Like everyone else, they watched with great interest. This time I turned my focus to Owen. He seemed to be checking out his surroundings, looking for an escape route, but he was out of luck.

"We were on Calico Peak the afternoon of the murder," Owen growled. "This woman should be arrested, and I'm going to call my lawyer about a libel suit."

"You never stepped foot on Calico Peak. Your entire alibi fell apart back there in our chat. There's no Buccaneer Trail and there's no lover's rock. Made all of it up."

Owen's laugh was pure evil. "You're basing all this on some stupid trick? You think you're so clever. We were hiking, and I just agreed to everything you asked because I wanted you to go away, you nosy woman."

"That's it, St. James. I've heard enough," Norwich said.

"Get out of the way." He motioned for the officer to take Aaron aboard the ferry.

"Sadie, that phone in your purse, Dirk's phone—"

"Who is Dirk?" Norwich asked.

I looked at Norwich in disbelief. "You're in the middle of a murder investigation and you know nothing about the second attack here on the island?"

Norwich waved his arm angrily. "How can I keep up with the incidents here on horror island?"

"Medics airlifted Dirk Evans off the island this morning. He'd been here all weekend with his drone, catching all kinds of footage of things that weren't supposed to be recorded." I looked pointedly at Sadie. "Dirk wasn't blackmailing you about your secret tryst with Theo. He had something much more valuable on his video feed." I turned to Owen. "Dirk's drone recorded the murder, and when Dirk saw what he had, he decided he could make some good money with a blackmail scheme. So, you attacked him with a rock and stole his phone." I turned to Norwich. "The stolen phone is in Sadie's purse."

Sadie held her purse close to her.

"Hand the evidence over," I told her. "It'll be the first step toward a more lenient sentence for your involvement in the murder."

"I had nothing to do with it," Sadie cried out. "It was all Owen. He gets so angry and jealous—" As she sobbed, she pulled the phone from her purse.

As Owen lunged at it, he let go of the parrot kite, which lifted into the air and floated majestically over the harbor before crash-landing into the waves. As it flew overhead, Sadie quickly threw the phone toward the crowd. Someone caught it and handed it over to Norwich.

Norwich looked suspiciously at the phone and then at me. I raised my eyebrows. "All the evidence of the murder—and Owen, the murderer—is in the drone video footage on that phone."

Norwich scowled at me. "You just couldn't stay out of this, could ya, St. James." He hesitated long enough to flare his nostrils my direction, then directed his officer to release Aaron and read Owen and Sadie their rights.

Wesley nodded at me. "You really are good at this."

I nodded back. "Thank you. And now I hope you all have a nice journey home."

The crowd cheered and clapped as I walked away from the dock. It was time to go home. Thank goodness. It had been a long day.

thirty-six

MY *FAMILY* INSISTED on cooking Sunday night dinner. Cora even managed to pull herself from her bed to help peel carrots. They'd decided on salads and cornbread, two things they all knew how to make.

Opal handed me a glass of wine. "Now take this somewhere comfortable and quiet and out of view of the chaos in the kitchen."

"This all sounds divine—except for the kitchen chaos part. Are you sure you don't want me—"

"No," they all said together.

"And take the handsome guy with the great smile along for your respite," Opal said. "He's not very good in the kitchen," she whispered loudly.

"Hey, I take offense to that," Nate said.

"At least you were the handsome guy with the great smile," Tobias said as he held up a knife in a way that any home economics teacher would scowl at.

I took Nate's hand. "Let's go. I don't mind that you're bad in the kitchen."

"I can make grilled cheese," he insisted as I pulled him out the back door. Huck rushed past us and pounced down to the river. The sun was setting and beautiful pastel pinks were smeared across the early evening sky.

Nate put his arm around my shoulder as I sipped my wine and stared out at the horizon. How many times I'd stared at the same horizon line, hoping and wishing that Michael's boat would suddenly appear.

A breeze pushed through the trees and ruffled my hair. I closed my eyes to absorb the refreshing smells of the island. Frostfall had more than its share of trouble, but I loved every inch of it. It was my home, and it was made more so by the people in the house (now wreaking havoc in my kitchen) and the man standing next to me.

I sighed.

"That sounded like a much-needed sigh," Nate said.

I turned to face him. "I keep thinking of a Mark Twain quote—'Apparently there is nothing that cannot happen today.' It's been one of those days—that's for darn sure."

"Hey, but you got the killer and put Norwich in his place…again."

"I'm still kind of stunned that I solved it. This was a tough one."

Nate smiled and kissed me lightly on the mouth. "I'm not stunned at all. I worked with a lot of crime experts in my time on the force, and none of them had your skills."

I rested my face against his chest, and he put his arms around me. "This is all I needed. Your arms around me."

We stood that way for a long moment. Frankly, I could have stayed like that for an hour, in his protective embrace, listening to his heartbeat and breathing in his soapy, manly scent.

I lifted my face, and we kissed. He lowered his arms, and we both turned toward the sunset again. The pinks were washing away, leaving behind a gray evening sky. "I'm trying to decide if this is it—if I've accepted that Michael is still alive and that he's been living an entirely different life all this time, or if it'll hit me all of a sudden and then I'll fall completely apart. I'm hoping it's the first one. I've already fallen apart over the man once. He doesn't get a second round."

"You're strong, Anna. I think you're right. It's the first one. All of us have things in our life that can make us stop occasionally and say, 'Wow, sometimes life is hard.' A wise man once said, 'Some days are diamonds and some days are rocks.'"

I smiled at him. "Tom Petty?"

He nodded. "You know, I think everything I've ever needed to know about life I learned from Tom Petty."

We both laughed. The past was over, and I had the present and it was fabulous. Some of the voices inside grew louder, Opal's the loudest of all. She was the self-appointed manager of the cooking team.

I turned to go find out what was happening.

"Finish your wine. I'll go put out the fire," Nate said. I

watched him stroll back to the house. He reached the steps. "And I can make a pretty good grilled cheese."

I lifted my glass of wine to him as he went inside. Huck's bark pulled my attention toward the river. The dog came trotting out of the shrubs. He stopped once, turned back toward the river and growled, then he shot past me to the house.

My adrenaline was pumping for the millionth time in this endless day. I stepped a little closer to the shrubs that bordered the river. "Michael?" I called into the dense foliage. There was no response. His boat had left the harbor. It couldn't be him.

I turned and walked to the house. I stopped and looked back once more. I didn't see anyone, but the hair on the back of my neck stood up just like Huck's. I was so done with this day. I opened the door and walked inside.

about the author

London Lovett is author of the Port Danby, Starfire, Firefly Junction, Scottie Ramone and Frostfall Island Cozy Mystery series. She loves getting caught up in a good mystery and baking delicious, new treats!

Learn more at:
www.londonlovett.com

Printed in Great Britain
by Amazon